A SOUND OF CHARIOTS

A SOUND OF CHARIOTS

MOLLIE HUNTER

HAMISH HAMILTON
London

*To Osyth Leeston,
in love, admiration, and gratitude;
and to the memory of
my parents, George and Ella McVeigh*

Printed Offset Litho and bound in Great
Britain by Cox & Wyman Ltd., London,
Fakenham and Reading

Part 1

1

The big black limousine gliding down the village street had the place to itself. It was a Sunday morning in September—too late in the season for weekend visitors to the sandy beach between the village and the Firth of Forth, too early in the morning for the Presbyterian natives of the village to be rising for their midmorning church service.

The driver of the car was uniformed, peak-capped; the passenger, a woman huddled down in a corner of the back seat. The car itself was an official one, shining, impeccable, almost soundless as it turned from the main street into a crescent of small semidetached houses boldly lettered, EARL HAIG HOUSING SCHEME FOR WAR VETERANS. It halted smoothly before the gate of one of them, but quietly as it arrived, it disturbed two of the houses into life.

At Number 4, a lifted lace curtain was dropped hurriedly back into place and a fat woman in a purplish print wrapper came hurrying out. From the back garden

3

of Number 3, the house at which the car had stopped, came the sound of voices, and as the woman passenger stepped out four children came running into view—three girls ranging in age from twelve to ten years and a five-year-old boy. They crowded towards the woman. She was unsteady on her feet and the fat woman supported her up the path to the front door of Number 3.

The driver's face watching them was anonymous as his plain black uniform. When they reached the front door he slid back under the steering wheel, and a fifth child, a girl who came hurrying from some far corner of the garden, was only just in time to see the car drive off. The sight of it abruptly checked her flight towards the door, but as soon as the smooth black back of the car had vanished round the bend of the crescent road she plunged into the house.

As she came into the kitchen a voice said, "Here's Bridie." After that there was no sound. The other children were huddled into a group by the window. They looked frightened. The child Bridie's glance swept past them to take in her mother and Mrs. Wallace from next door standing by the fireplace, and the neighbour's presence registered as strange for she knew that her mother disliked Mrs. Wallace. A chill of uneasiness ran over her and the picture presented by the two women focused suddenly in her vision with unnatural clarity of detail.

Her mother had her outdoor clothes on, but her hat was tilted crookedly to one side so that her hair straggled down her cheeks. She was standing in a curious way, with one hand pressed to her side, and straining backwards as if she had hurt her back. Her face was flushed. The skin looked shiny and tight over her cheekbones but round her eyes it was puffed-up and tender-looking as if she had been crying for a long time, and she was looking at them all and yet beyond them as if they had been made of glass.

Mrs. Wallace was crying. Tears were oozing out of the little pale blue eyes sunk deep behind the fat of her cheeks. They swam in the sockets till there was enough of them to spill over the pads of fat and trickle down her face, and it crossed Bridie's mind that this must be an uncomfortable way to cry, for Mrs. Wallace made no attempt to wipe away the oozing, trickling tears. She stood so still that she was like the statue of a fat woman crying.

Her arms were folded and resting on the big bulge of her stomach—great slabs of arms mottled all red and blue with weather and the washtub, and as Bridie stared at them, Mrs. Wallace's hands came slowly to life. They wandered over her upper arms, the fingers aimlessly picking and rubbing at the mottled skin. The watery blue eyes rolled round to rest on Bridie and William and the Others.

"Puir bairns," she said.

The words were only a whisper of sound. Her breath came out in a long quivering sigh; at the end of it, then she shook her head and repeated hoarsely, "Puir bairns. Puir bairns."

5

Bridie felt the sharpness of perception that had photographed the scene slip away into a fog of bewilderment, and through the blur of her thoughts she heard her mother say,

"I'll have to tell them."

Her voice sounded thick and breathless as if she was frightened. Mrs. Wallace gave a gulping sob and looked away from them. A fuzziness began to grow in Bridie's head and through it her mother's voice came again,

"Your father's dead."

Her voice seemed to go round and round like an echo in a cave. Bridie heard it booming in her head and she became confused trying to sort this out. The voice was in her head echoing round and round . . . the echo was in a cave . . . her head was a cave . . . Then the booming in her head sharpened in pitch and steadied to the shrill focus of William's voice screaming.

Her mother was trying to explain "dead" to him but William wouldn't listen. He kept shouting, *"When's my da comin' back? When's he comin' back?"* and screaming with temper because she wouldn't tell him when.

He was purple in the face with temper, kicking and beating his fists against their mother and Bridie was angry with her for not seeing that such a little boy couldn't understand "dead," and sorry for her because she was crying so much. She thought guiltily that it was herself who should be trying to quiet William because looking after him was one of the things that divided herself and William from the Others. But something seemed to have happened to her legs. She couldn't move.

The fuzziness began to come back to her head. Then it seemed that the fuzziness was in the room, making everything wobble and take queer shapes. The room was all muddled with people talking and moving about and there was a sound of sobbing. She wondered if it was herself crying and put her hand up to her eyes but there were no tears there.

Quite suddenly after that, there was only Aileen and herself in the kitchen with her mother, and Aileen was asking,

"Will Bridie and me not go with the Sunday papers, then?"

Aileen was ten, a year older than her, and she was the clever one of the family as well, but this seemed to Bridie a silly question. You didn't go out delivering papers the morning your father died just as if it was an ordinary morning, did you?

"I don't *want* to go with the papers," she said quickly, and with surprise saw the disapproval on her mother's face.

"I don't think we should let Mr. Purves down," her mother said.

"But my daddy's—"

"Get your coat on, Bridie." Her mother wasn't listening to her. "You know it's selfish to let people down."

She turned to follow Aileen then, with the usual flush of guilt and shame creeping up her back. She did know it was selfish of course, and she knew that selfishness

7

was wicked. It was only for the moment she had forgotten things like that. Yet still through the excuses forming in her mind came a stab of the old nightmare fear in which her mother was safely inside the Golden Gate while she was shut out of Heaven with all the other wicked people. She panicked from the needle of fear, running down the garden path and along the road, struggling into her coat as she ran, and pretending she was in a hurry to reach the paper-shop.

She was too early. The shop door was shut and the blind was still drawn. The papers hadn't arrived yet. She leaned against the shop door till Aileen came up and sat on the bench outside the shop, then she went across and sat beside her. Aileen didn't speak but her presence there seemed to make time real again for the two of them. Outside of herself and Aileen sitting on the bench there was nothing—no world, nothing happening, no time. Time had stopped in that moment of sharp awareness of her mother and Mrs. Wallace standing beside the fireplace.

In the time that existed between herself and Aileen she became conscious that the bench was too high for her. Her feet were dangling uncomfortably above the ground and there was something wrong with her stomach. She remembered that they had had no breakfast, but that wasn't what was wrong because she wasn't hungry. She looked at Aileen, wishing she would say something, but her sister had the closed look on her face that meant she didn't want to talk. The strange feeling

8

in her inside got worse and she said, trying the word out cautiously,

"Aileen . . ."

Aileen didn't answer. She looked straight ahead, sitting hunched up with her feet lined neatly side by side on the pavement and her hands squashed down into her coat pockets.

"Aileen," Bridie tried again. "I'm cold."

Aileen turned her head then. Her face was plump and round as a button like it always was, but now Bridie could see the bones of it standing out through the softness of her cheeks, and there were deep lines running down from her nose to the corners of her mouth. Through the shock of her surprise she thought, "That's how Aileen will look when she's old!," and heard her speaking in the cold, clear voice she used when she was afraid Bridie was going to make a show of herself. Aileen hated a show.

"There's nobody but us will care about him being dead," Aileen said.

"I'm not going to cry, honest I'm not," Bridie said, and she tried to explain about the cold feeling in her inside, as if her inside was gone and there was nothing there except cold air, cold, cold, cold, in her stomach and in her head. But the words came out all mixed up and sounding stupid and Aileen turned her head away without answering.

A few people went by after that. Then the van that brought the papers down from Edinburgh drew up

9

outside the shop. Mr. Purves came out and went over to the van, going step-hop, step-hop, on the wooden leg he had because of The War. He came back carrying the bundles of papers and shouted to them,

"When's your dad comin' home from the hospital then, lassies?"

Aileen said, "My dad's dead," and Mr. Purves stopped in the middle of a step-hop. His round, gooseberry eyes opened so wide that a white circle showed round each of them, then he looked away with one hand tugging at the ends of his spiky moustache. He began to say something, then he coughed and went back into the shop without finishing what he had been going to say.

The slip-slop of the papers being folded sounded from the shop for a while before Aileen got up from the bench. Bridie followed her into the shop. Mr. Purves was standing behind the counter pushing the folded papers into the big canvas bags for herself and Aileen to carry. Mrs. Purves was there too, with her hair all messed up and her eyes watering as if she had just got out of bed.

"Get the bairns a glass of lemonade, Jock," she said to Mr. Purves.

The Purveses were mean. They never usually gave herself or Aileen anything, but Aileen said, "No, thank you," quickly before Mr. Purves could move.

Mrs. Purves took a box of biscuits off a shelf. "Well, here's a nice biscuit tae ye, then." She was smiling at them but her lips were shaking so that the smile was all twisted.

10

"We don't want anything, thank you," Aileen said. She took one canvas bag off the counter and Bridie reached up for the other one. It was heavy and she had to walk slowly with it to where the message-bikes were leaning against the outside wall of the shop. Aileen was off before her because she was held up again by the effort of swinging the bag into the wicker carrier on the front of the bike. The sound of Mr. and Mrs. Purves talking came out through the open door while she was steadying the bike. It sounded as if they were quarrelling and she heard Mr. Purves shouting,

". . . and they're a right unnatural pair of bairns if you ask me! No' a tear shed atween them!"

Mrs. Purves shouted back at him, "Ye damn great fool—did ye no' see yon Bridie's face?" Then in a quieter voice she said, "McShane shouldna have favoured Bridie sae much above his ither bairns. She'll break her heart for him, poor wee soul."

Their voices came to Bridie the way she remembered hearing things in sick, daytime dreams, now booming far away, now close up and sharp so that they hurt her ears. Mr. Purves' voice came close up suddenly, sounding right against her ear.

"Ach, she'll soon forget. She's ower young to remember much aboot him onywey."

The hard, confident voice jabbed in her eardrum like a finger poked painfully into a tender spot. The pain of it shot behind her brow and darted into her eyes. Her eyes were stinging. They were wet. Blindly through her tears she fumbled with her foot for the pedal. Her weight pressed it down and she was swinging forward and up on to the seat of the bicycle as it jerked into motion. Then she was wobbling out into the road and the bicycle was gathering speed down the hill away from the paper-shop.

The air was rushing past her, sucked into her lungs and blurted out again in great heaving sobs that filled her throat with retching, choking pain. Then the pain burst outwards from her and she was howling through the rush of wind, howling like an animal in the unbearable pain and desolation of understanding at last that her father was dead.

2

Bridie's first memory of her father was a very clear one.

First came the sound of his voice in a deep rumbling chuckle beside her ear and the looming-up of his presence between her and the light. Then came the warm hard grasp of his hands spanning her chest, and the stomach-dropping thrill of being lifted high into the air. She swung above him half-screaming, half-laughing with terror and delight, his face beneath her a brief mysterious vision of shining planes and shadowed hollows, of brows tip-tilted over laughter-glittering eyes and light striking off the white gleam of teeth; and in the instant of glimpsing it over the swinging void between them was suddenly and vividly aware of the strength that held her.

Confidence surged into her, stiffening the muscles of her back and legs. For a fleeting moment she was tense and fearless, gloriously poised for flight above him while he said through laughter,

"You can have the other bairns, Agnes. *This one's mine!*"

Then he brought her hurtling down, breathless and laughing with him in the backwash of pleasure from the glory of the flying moment.

The memory finished sharply at this point so that she knew it must belong to her baby days before she could remember faces and voices and conversations all properly connected up like a story, which was how she liked to think about things. There were other memories that she knew must belong to those days because they were isolated in the same way in her mind, like pictures without frames spaced out on a blank wall—a wall that ended abruptly on the day William was born. She was four and a half years older than William so that she could date exactly from this the day when memory began to open out in one clear continuous picture in her mind.

That morning began with waking to the recollection that it was her turn to run downstairs and creep in beside her mother in the big brass bed that stood in one corner of the kitchen. She scuttled down the stairs, her bare toes curling back from the cold feel of the linoleum and anticipation tingling up her back at the thought of burrowing into her mother's warmth. In the dim morning light her mother was a humped form in the bed, a hump that unexpectedly stretched out an arm to bar her scramble under the covers.

"Not this morning, Bridie," she said. "There's a baby

14

in the bed this morning—a boy! Look!"

And then while she stood staring in confusion at the shawl-shrouded knob of a face held out for her to see, her mother added.

"You've lost your place in the sun, Bridie."

Her voice was high with a break in it that could have been either a laugh or a sob, and for some reason she did not understand then it touched off in Bridie's mind a vivid recollection of her father saying triumphantly, *"This one's mine!"* She was still struggling to grasp the link between this earliest memory of her father and the words, *"You've lost your place in the sun, Bridie,"* when the Others came tumbling down the stairs and she was caught up in the excitement of their discovery of the new baby. Her voice soared up to join the clamour of her sisters' tongues, and because her mother's eyes were still so strangely fixed on her she tried to cover up her discomfiture by shouting and boasting louder than they did that now she had a baby brother.

The moment stayed fixed in her mind as the time-point at which she became actively aware of her relationship to the rest of the family. Suddenly she was no longer just herself, Bridie, she was also Bridie the fourth child and youngest daughter in the McShane family and sister of the new baby, the boy William. But she was not glad, as she pretended to be, that she had a baby brother. She was afraid of the mystery of her mother's words and uneasy at the link they had made with her first memory of her father, and the uneasiness stayed with her so that she became alert to any word or look that might help to explain it.

Mostly it was when her mother and Mrs. Soutar were having tea that scraps of information came her way. Mrs. Soutar had no children and she had bad nerves. She took long walks every day for her bad nerves and usually on her way home she stopped in at their house for a cup of tea, and over tea she talked about her nerves and another of her troubles called "miscarriages," and Bridie's mother talked about the Others and Bridie and William being born.

By the time she had grasped the burden of these conversations she had also learned the value of her mother's description of her as being "deaf as a post when she has her nose in a book." On the occasions she was present during Mrs. Soutar's visits, therefore, she sat very quietly behind her book, and over the next year or so she collected a surprising amount of information for, as she was to discover later, she had the power of almost total recall of speech and the printed word. At this time, however, she was only aware of screeds of words being photographed on her mind and of the difficulty of sorting from these the ones she could understand, and because of this her mind was apt to drift off from the conversation when it caught hold of some familiar word or name —like that of Dr. McLaren, for instance.

Mrs. Soutar mentioned him one day when she was talking about the new young doctor who had just come to the village. She liked him. She said he was a perfect gentleman when he examined you, and then she said, "Why do you always have that old McLaren down from Edinburgh for your confinements, Agnes? I don't know how you stand the coarse old devil."

"Oh aye, he's coarse all right," her mother said. "He swears like a trooper—words I wouldn't soil my lips with except to tell you, Lena. But he's been my doctor since I was a wee lassie, after all, and that sort of gives you confidence in a man if you know what I mean. My own mother swears by him and she should know—he's birthed seven for her!"

She was so busy thinking about Dr. McLaren by this time that the next bit of the conversation went over her head. Dr. McLaren fascinated her. He was so tall and thin that when she looked up at him his grey suit seemed to go on stretching in wrinkles above her forever. Then, just as she was thinking there couldn't be any more of him she would come to his face, all wrinkled like his suit with cheeks like hard red apples and above them two of the bluest eyes she had ever seen. They sparked, those eyes! Tiny and blue and fierce they sparked under the grey cliff of his eyebrows, and above them the deep lines on his forehead went up in steps to the bush of soft white hair standing out round his head like the floss on a dandelion.

The Others were frightened of Dr. McLaren because of the way he shouted at people, but she was always too interested in his appearance to be frightened. Once she had twisted her ankle and her father had said to her when he was taking her up to Edinburgh to see Dr. McLaren, "No tears now, Bridie. McLaren's bark is worse than his bite and I don't like cowards," so that she had gone into the surgery with him determined not to cry even if McLaren did hurt her.

When they came in Dr. McLaren said, "Well, Patrick, I did my best with the Ministry but they won't raise your pension. You're still a twenty per cent disability on their blasted books."

Her father said, "Did you tell them about the dizzy spells?" and Dr. McLaren said, "Aye, but I might have been shouting down a well for all the satisfaction I got."

Her father sat down with his head in his hands and Dr. McLaren took a bottle out of a drawer in his desk and said, "Come on, Patrick, we'll have a dram. Nothin' like a dram for drinking damnation to mealy-mouthed pen-pushers that never had a smell of the trenches, eh?" Then he poured some of the stuff from the bottle into two glasses and they began to talk.

It was all about the Great World War and she listened for a while but her ankle was hurting her so much that she had to start counting to keep her mind off it. By the time Dr. McLaren was ready to look at it she felt like crying again and when he lifted her foot on to his knee and shouted at her, "What the hell did ye want to go and do a damn silly thing like that for?" she nearly did cry with the pain and the fright he gave her. That made her angry because she had been so determined not to cry in front of her father and she shouted back at him,

"I'm not goin' to cry for you, see! My mam says you're just an old bully anyway!"

Dr. McLaren laughed then and so did her father, the two of them laughing so hard that they rocked back and forward in their chairs, and Dr. McLaren shouted,

"By God, that's a well-plucked 'un, Patrick! You're dam' right—she *is* every bit as good as a laddie!"

It was the remembrance of this remark that brought her attention sharply back to the conversation between her mother and Mrs. Soutar. The day William was born had something to do with what Dr. McLaren had said to her father about her that day. Something had clicked in her mind so that she understood that now.

"You remember the snow that fell the night William was born, Lena," her mother was saying, "and how old McLaren's car got stuck in a drift so that he had to walk the last three miles here? Well, that started him. He was swearing and cursing like mad when he got here, then the scullery door stuck when the nurse was passing out the hot water to him and he yelled at me as if it was my fault, 'Dammit woman, is there nothin' goes right in this bloody house?'

"Patrick was pacing up and down outside the door and he yelled out to him, 'Ye're wastin' shoe leather, Patrick. She's only good for havin' lassies, this one!'

"I'm telling you, if I'd had my strength I'd have smacked his face for him—but it's funny too, it was a real comfort in a way to have him there bawling his head off as usual. And mind you, he's a real good doctor for all his bad language. He knew right away that William was going to be a breech birth and you wouldn't have believed how gentle he was, calling me his 'bonnie lassie' and his 'good wee hen' and foolishness like that before he put me under the chloroform."

Bridie forgot about pretending not to listen at this point. Her mother was wonderful at telling stories, with her face and her voice changing all the time so that she looked and sounded like the person who was supposed to be talking, and her hands making gestures that drew pictures of everything that was happening.

"I was just coming out of the chloroform," she said in her own voice, "and the bairn was only halfway born when I heard that old devil shouting"—her voice went cracked and deep like Dr. McLaren's voice and her face scrunched up into his malicious old gnome's grin—" 'It's a boy, Patrick! By God, it's a boy at last!' "

Mrs. Soutar t'ch t'ched loudly and Bridie's mother gave a little laugh. "Patrick had his ear glued to the door," she said, "and I didn't know it then but McLaren told me afterwards that the words were hardly out of his mouth before he was running up through the snow to the manse to register William's birth. One o'clock in the morning in the middle of a snow storm he knocked the minister up out of his bed! That'll give you an idea of how badly he'd wanted a son."

There was fussing about filling up the teapot after that and a lot of talk about things that weren't part of the story. Then Bridie's mother said suddenly,

"You know the favourite he's always made of Bridie—all that nonsense about her being as good as a son. I'd have sworn that William's birth would have put an end to that but—"

Bridie sensed the breaking-off of the sentence before her mother checked the next word. It was part of the game of listening quietly. You learned to tell just when they had noticed you again and then you had to make it look as if you hadn't been listening. In the flash of time before her mother's eyes turned to rest on her she lowered her head so that her nose was almost on the print of her book, and when her mother spoke to her she waited a moment before she looked up vacantly and said "What?"

"I said, 'Go and tell the Others it's time for their tea,' " her mother repeated so sharply that Bridie knew she must have thought she was too deep in her book to have heard the conversation.

She went out into the garden to call her sisters. "Nell! Aileen! Moira!" she shouted, and as she called their names she was thinking how her mother had referred to them as "the Others." That was always how she thought of them in her own mind and sometimes she had wondered vaguely how this had come about. Now she knew. All the gaps were filled in. Her father had wanted a boy and he had got four girls instead, but he had thought she was just as good as a boy and so she had become his favourite. That was what her mother had meant by

21

her place in the sun—but she had been wrong that morning for she hadn't lost it when William was born. She was still the one her father took for walks on Saturdays. It was still her he took riding on the carrier of his bicycle. She was still his favourite even though he was so pleased and proud to have William, and later when William was old enough, she would share her place in the sun with him.

The tide of excitement rising in her at the discovery made her want to laugh and shout and race about. She began to tumble about on the grass, turning somersaults and then jumping up to swing on the lowest branch of the cherry tree. The Others saw her as they came up from the foot of the garden.

"Bridie's capering again," Aileen said scornfully. That was always what they said when she tumbled about and shouted to let the excitement out of her, but she didn't care. She shouted defiance at them and Nell shouted back, "You come down from there, Bridie Mc-Shane! You know fine you're not allowed to swing on the cherry tree!"

Mrs. Soutar came out and went down the path. The Others went in and her mother called to her from the house but Bridie went on swinging. Faster and faster, her voice rising with every swing to a whoop that defied the punishing rasp of the branch against the skin of her palms; higher and higher till the leaves of the tree were like a green storm above her head with shards of sky

22

flashing through it like blue lightning. Faster and higher still till her head and the green storm and the blue lightning exploded simultaneously into a million whirling colours and she was flying through the air and landing with a great bruising crash in the rose-bed.

She felt sick, picking herself up out from the tearing thorns of the rose bushes. She blinked her eyes, trying to steady the garden spinning round her and saw her father watching her as he latched the gate behind him.

"I was swinging on the cherry tree," she said, following his look to the long tear in her dress. She rubbed her hands down her skirt to take the earth from them, then straightened up and faced him steadily. He would forgive anything except a lie. She knew that. There was no punishment bad enough for a lie. She watched his face, trying to judge what he would say.

"You'd better show yourself to your mother," he told her.

His face wasn't smiling but his eyes were and she went in slowly and offered herself for inspection, not saying anything but relying on his presence behind her because of the smile she had seen in his eyes.

The argument went on over her head, most of it familiar, most of it in her mother's voice, ". . . the cost of clothes . . . always rampaging around like a boy . . . too wild for her own good . . ." Grunts and little exclamations from her father, then a loud voice—the voice no one argued with,

"You've got the remedy in your own hands, Agnes. If she behaves like a boy, dress her like a boy. Now that's an end of it."

His hand came down on her shoulder. "And while your hands are dirty you can clean my leggings for me. Come on, Miss Malloy. March!"

"It's Sergeant McGra for marching," she corrected him, twisting her head back to look at him as he marched her into the scullery.

Her father had all sorts of names for her as well as Sergeant McGra and Miss Malloy but sometimes he forgot the right order of them. Miss Malloy was her polite company name. He grinned down at her now as he handed her the brushes. "Right, Sergeant McGra it is. Polish parade just now, Sergeant, and then you won't have to turn to it in the morning."

He put his foot up on the wooden top of the brush-box and she began to polish the black leather legging that encased his leg from ankle to knee. This was her job, polishing his leggings every morning, and always as she rubbed away at them she thought of the story in the Bible of the blind man that Jesus healed and what he said to the people who asked him what he saw when his eyes were opened.

"I saw men like trees walking."

That was what her father was like towering above her as she polished the great black column of his legging. Strong and powerful and taller than people—like a tree walking.

24

Presently when she began on the second legging she remembered William, and gasping a little over it because polishing was hard work she asked, "Dad, will we take William on the bike with us when he's bigger?"

"We will and all," her father said.

A doubt struck her, slowing down the rub-rub of the polishing cloth in her hand. "Where will he sit, though? There's not room on the carrier for two of us."

He rubbed his chin, pretending to consider, but his eyes were twinkling and she knew he was only teasing. She hopped with impatience all the same and laughing at her antics he said, "I'll make a wee saddle to fix on to the bar of the bike. William can sit on that and hold on to the middle bit of the handlebars and you'll still have the carrier to yourself."

She thought it was a perfect arrangement and finished the polishing in a burst of energy that drew grunts of approval from him. Then, in a glow of achievement, she went off to the bathroom to wash the earth and polish off her hands. She ran the water, singing through the sound of it, but not too loud in case God heard her. It was a hymn she was singing, and it was all right to sing hymns loudly in Sunday school because then she thought properly about God. But not when she sang them at home by herself, because then she deliberately thought of the *He* in the hymns as her father, and if God found that out there would be even less chance of her getting into Heaven than there was before she had invented this pleasure for herself.

3

Bridie thought a great deal about God but her feelings on the subject were very mixed. God was very useful when she had to go upstairs in the dark by herself, because He was so powerful that He could get there to save her before the bogles jumped out to catch her at the darkest bend of the stairs. On the other hand, God was Merciless. He was also the Wrath to Come, and the Great Judge, and she was uneasily aware that she was Unworthy to be Saved.

Her mother was Saved because she had been Washed in the Blood of the Lamb when she was a member of the Brethren in Edinburgh before she was married. She had told them all about this, and it seemed to Bridie a very good way of dealing with the problem of Heaven and Hell.

The Brethren didn't have churches, they had meeting-houses instead. The Sinners sat on one side of the meeting-house and the Saints sat on the other, and if you were a Sinner you just waited till the Spirit visited you then you stood up and said you wanted to be Saved. That was when you were Washed in the Blood of the Lamb and crossed over to sit with the Saints. After that you were all right; you were sure to go to Heaven.

Her mother was very anxious for them all to be Saved like herself, but there was no meeting-house in the village where they could go and sit with the Sinners so they all went to Sunday school instead. They didn't Save you there but at least, her mother said, they taught you the Scriptures and that was something.

Bridie didn't feel it was enough. She had so many sins to her account like Reading Secular Literature on the Sabbath and Lack of Consideration for Others, that she was sure it was long odds against her getting into Heaven. She knew about odds because her father had explained it to her from the racing paper he got every Saturday to pick out the name of the horse he was going to back to win enough money to go home to Ireland and take them all with him. He had also explained to her why odds were long on some horses and short on others, and on her seventh birthday she decided it would shorten the odds on her getting to Heaven if she went to church as well as Sunday school. So she began to go to church every Sunday and discovered that she liked it very much.

When the hymns were sung she liked to hear the dark richness of the men's voices growling deep under the quavering sweetness of the women's singing. She enjoyed singing, herself, the hymns with tunes like music

27

marching into battle; but her favourites were the ones that had mourning in the music for, as she sang these, she could feel being drawn out of her a feeling of longing, a great and terrible yearning for something she could not name and which she knew she would never reach. It was a strange and painful feeling, this yearning, yet still it was more desirable than any pleasure, and sometimes it gripped her so strongly that the tears came from nowhere and ran down her face. After that the feeling would ease off, but if old Miss Nelson who sat next to her noticed her tears, she would lean over and give her a pan drop which she kept to suck during the sermon.

Next to the hymns she liked the readings from the Bible—which were not the little quiet stories from the New Testament they read in Sunday school. In church the minister read from the Old Testament, terrible tales of kings and queens and wars and prophets, and in her mind's eye she saw them all, brazen and brilliant and vividly alive. Jezebel, with scarlet and gold sumptuous against her copper skin and heavy painted lids hooding the secret pagan thoughts in her slanted eyes; and Ahab, her husband, the weak cruelty of his greedy face half-masked by the black of his spade-shaped beard. She saw the Hosts of the Lord breaking over arid battle-plains in brass-bright waves of shields and helmets, with thousands of shining swords held erect like the rays of some great jewel stabbing upward to the burning blue of the sky. She shivered under the beat of the blue-black wings of Elijah's ravens, fearing the cruel beaks

that held the prophet's food; she saw the fatal strands
of Absalom's hair twisted horribly around the whiteness
of his throat and chokingly shared the agony and terror
of his death, so that when the Bible-reading was finished she was sometimes glad of the respite of the sermon when she could suck her pan drop and study the
rest of the people in the church.

It was looking around her like this that first made her
realize how the village was divided into three separate
sections, each with a different kind of people in it. First
of all were the people who really belonged to the village,
like the farm-workers in the Tied Houses and the black-
smith, the grocer and the postmistress—the sort of people who had lived there even before the Great World
War. Then there were the English. Her father said they
were not really English, they just spoke yaw-yaw like
English people because they were ashamed of their na-
tive Scottish heritage. They lived in the big houses down
by the sea—which wasn't a sea but the firth or mouth
of the River Forth. She had learned that at geography.
The English had cars and servants and they called people by their last names without any "mister" which she
thought was rude.

Then there were the people from her own street, the
War Veterans' houses, but not many of them came to
church except on Armistice Sunday when the men pa-
raded wearing their medals. There was Mr. Blair and
Mr. Bruce and Mr. Wilson who were blind. Mr. Corbett
and Mr. Purves and Mr. Wallace each had a wooden leg.

Mr. Fraser had no arms, and Mr. Muir had no legs. Mr. Miller had no arms either and he was blind as well but they all came on Armistice Sunday except for Mr. Telfer and Mr. Souness who had gone mad from shell shock and been taken off to the Asylum, and old Murphy who never left his wheelchair and said there was no God anyway, and her father who said that old Murphy was a fool but that the church was a serious obstacle to social enlightenment.

Bridie had no idea what social enlightenment was but she knew it must be important because her father was very serious when he talked about it, and so she brought up the subject to Mr. Gladsmuir the minister when he was speaking to her one day after church. He often spoke to her because she came so regularly, and since he was the one who was in charge of the church she felt it was up to him to stop it being an obstacle to social enlightenment.

Mr. Gladsmuir stroked his moustache and looked at her very oddly over his hand all the time she was talking and then he asked,

‹ "How old are you, my child?"

"I'm seven," Bridie told him, and to make it sound more important she added, "but I'll be eight soon. My birthday's in July."

"Well, I'm seventy-one years old," Mr. Gladsmuir said. "That's ten times your age, my dear, so you can take it that I know what I'm talking about."

His face became very stern. "The boot is on the other

foot," he said. "It is your father's views that present a serious obstacle to his own Salvation. I will pray for him, my child, and you must add your prayers to mine. Remember the words of Isaiah, '*And a little child shall lead them.*'"

He patted her shoulder and went slowly off to the vestry, shaking his head and frowning, and Bridie went home considerably disturbed by the conversation. Her father was not Saved, after all, because he was not a member of the Brethren, and apart from that going to church was the only other way she knew of getting into Heaven. What was the point then of her striving to get there if he was going to be left out?

It was not even as if she wanted to go to Heaven for the pleasure of it—after all, what was there to *do* in Heaven once you had been given your Robe of White and Crown of Gold? It was only the fear of being separated from her mother on the Day of Judgment that had driven her so far, and now that she was faced with the knowledge that there was no way for her father to get to Heaven it struck her that she might have to choose eventually between Heaven with her mother or Outer Darkness with her father.

It was a prospect she could not bear to face. Somehow, she thought, she would have to persuade her father to change his views to agree with the minister's. It was the only way of making sure that the three of them would be safely together inside the Golden Gate when the time came. However, it was difficult to decide ex-

31

actly what to say to him and it was not till the Saturday evening following her conversation with Mr. Gladsmuir that she saw an opportunity to open the matter.

She came into the kitchen shortly before bedtime that day, and found her mother laying out clean clothes for everyone for Sunday and her father getting ready to go out to the Parish Meeting. Her mother took a clean shirt off the clothes-horse for him as she came in, and turning round with it in her hand said,

"A little less politics and a lot more religion would do you a world of good, Patrick. You'd be far better down on your knees praying for the souls of those in the village than trying to force Socialism down their throats."

"You could get to Heaven with praying too, Dad," Bridie said quickly in case this golden opportunity for opening her argument slipped away.

Her father had been shaving and he was still looking in the mirror as he dabbed his face dry. His eyes slid sideways and down to her. "Bridie," he asked, "who was Jesus Christ?" and obediently she recited, "Jesus was the Son of God. He came to save us from our sins."

"I'll tell you something else about him," her father said. "Christ was a revolutionary."

"Patrick!" That was her mother, her voice rising up in a shriek of horror, and quickly, in case she wasn't allowed to hear any more, she asked,

"What's a revol—what you said?"

"You're not to be blasphemous in front of that child," her mother said sternly. "I forbid it."

Bridie waited for the explosion. Nobody used words like "forbid" to her father. But there was no explosion. Her father turned away from the mirror and put his hands on her mother's shoulders.

"Agnes," he said, "I know you'd face lions for your faith. But it's *your* faith, remember. Don't try to force it on me."

He spoke quite patiently and Bridie was relieved. Then he knelt down on one knee beside her and put his arm round her waist.

"A revolutionary is someone who wants to change the way things are run," he explained, "and that's what Christ tried to do. He tried to put the rule of love in place of the fear of kings and priests and tax-gatherers. That's why they killed him, Bridie, for all these priests and tax-gatherers and so on were only concerned with power and riches, and they knew very well there would be no place for such things in a kingdom of love. They were afraid for their moneybags, Bridie girl, and when people are frightened they become cruel. So they killed him, Bridie; they killed the gentle revolutionary who tried to drive the greed from men's hearts and bring in glory."

The picture of Christ crucified—nails in the tender flesh, thorns stabbing the defeated head—was too terrible to carry in her mind. Quickly she blotted it out with the spread of white blazing wings in the empty Easter sepulchre and argued aloud to convince herself,

"It was all right, though. He rose again at Easter."

"Of course He did, it says so in the Bible," her mother said. "No one can really kill God, Bridie."

"Or the little spark of the divine in man." Her father rose as he spoke and stood gazing over her head. She looked for greater reassurance in his eyes but they were looking past her to some point far away.

"Such a little light to live by," he said, "and how hard the system tries to smother it."

Her mother handed him his shirt. "You'll be late," she warned. He took it from her, his mind coming back from the distance and remembering.

"The world is no better now than it was in Christ's time, Bridie," he said, "and it won't change till everyone is prepared to fight for truth and justice. Remember that. We've got to be revolutionaries, like Christ, if we want a better world."

"Are you that—what you said?" she asked.

Her father gave a grim little laugh. "In this neck of the woods it's a bad word," he said, "but yes, Bridie, I am. I am a revolutionary."

He pulled his shirt over his head. Watching as his head poked out at her through the front of the shirt, Bridie wasn't sure that she had understood what he had told her but she smiled at him to let him think she did understand. He smiled back at her, a wide grin that stretched his brown face into a big, laughing mask, and suddenly her heart was so light that she felt as if she was a balloon ready to fly up into the air.

Laughing back at him she said excitedly, stumbling

34

over the long word, "I'm a revol—revolutionary too, then!"

Her mother began to talk again but her father drowned what she said with his shout, "That's the stuff, my girl! Up the revolution, and we'll both ride to Heaven on Marx's coat-tails."

He was still laughing when her mother seized her and hustled her out of the kitchen so that she had no chance to ask who Marx was. But thinking it over in bed that night she decided that, whoever he was, it would be much more exciting to ride to Heaven on his coat-tails than to get there by crossing over from the Sinners to the Saints.

The thought of it kept her awake long after Moira had fallen asleep beside her that night and the whispering of Nell and Aileen in the other bed in the big front room had faded into silence. She heard the front door slam behind her father when he went out to the meeting and later, just as she was beginning to drift off to sleep, the faint sound from the kitchen of her mother playing the harmonium.

The music sounded in her ear pressed to the pillow like the faraway humming of a giant bumblebee. *"Jesu, lover of my soul,"* droned the bumblebee, *"Let me to Thy bosom fly . . ."*

Her mother's voice rose up, sweetly encased inside the droning murmur. *"Hide me, O my Saviour, hide, Till the storm of life is past . . ."*

When the music was finished her mother would go

out, too, to the Parish Hall, and wait outside it for her father in case he got hurt when he was thrown out of the meeting. He wouldn't keep being thrown out, she said, if he didn't insist on getting up on the platform and telling them a lot of things they didn't want to hear. Then they got angry, shouting up at him, their faces all upturned—dark, bearded faces, long-nosed, cruel-lined, yelling *"Crucify him! Crucify him!"* They shook fists at him, the gentle revolutionary still trembling from the torture of the whips and the thorns. They followed him, jeering, on the Calvary road and stretched him out against the Cross, and pity for the agony of the nails shook her so that she could not bear to watch.

But still she saw the outline of the Cross rise slowly against the darkened sky and looking up she saw his face, her father's face staring down in voiceless anguish at her from under the crown of thorns. She tried to cry out in protest but the sound would not come from her throat and desperately struggling to voice it she found herself sitting upright in bed.

Darkness danced in front of her eyes and the room was full of the sound of the Others breathing. She sat rigid in shock, only gradually becoming aware that she had slept and that the horrifying confusion in her mind of her father with Christ had been a dream.

In the reassurance of familiar things the sharp outline of horror round her dream faded, and the quick bellows-pumping of her breath slackened its pace. Her rigid pose relaxed but the effect of the dream was still with her,

and wide-awake now, she sat thinking uneasily of her
father at the Parish Meeting.

They couldn't crucify him of course; people didn't get
crucified nowadays. But suppose they put him in jail?
They might hang him then—some people in jail did get
hanged. . . .

Unable to bear the thought she covered it up in action,
slipping out of bed and going quietly on tiptoe across
the front room out to the stair-landing that gave on to
the little back room. She could see across the fields to
the Parish Hall from the window of the back room and
she settled down beside it, crouching low against the
sill so that she could tuck the hem of her nightgown
round her bare feet.

The dark shape of the hall was chequered with shining yellow squares, with a bar of light falling also from
the transom over the door, and once her eyes became
accustomed to the pattern of light and shade she was
able to distinguish the waiting form of her mother standing just within the range of the transom light. Somehow
she had almost expected to see the building move and
shake with the violence of feeling it housed, but the lit
windows were the only sign of life in it.

She grew cold, crouched on the draughty floor, too cold
eventually to stir or change her position. Her thoughts
became a slow, meaningless procession imaging the ob-
jects within view—the hall, her mother, the ruled dark
line of hedges and the bunched deep dark of the tree-tops
against the silver-spotted dark of the sky. In the grip of

this stupor she was slow at first to notice the figures that began to appear in silhouette against the lit windows, and by the time she had realized their presence the silhouettes were in motion, wavering back and forth in angry gestures directed towards one end of the hall.

The mime spread from window to window till each square of light had its gesturing silhouette, and suddenly the door flew open, crashing so violently back on its hinges that the sound carried to her across the fields. A body came hurtling out and landed in the path of light from the door. She saw her mother go down beside it in a swift kneeling motion, and as quickly regain her feet again to come between the body and the men crowding through the doorway. There was a brief confusion of milling figures round the door that resolved itself into men retreating back into the hall and two intertwined figures moving slowly away from it.

The door of the hall closed and she waited, knowing how long it would take her father and mother to walk home. Then painfully straightening her cramped legs, she rose when she heard the front door open. A murmur of voices came from downstairs and when they were cut off again by the closing of the kitchen door behind them, she crept quietly out of the back room and began a cautious descent of the stairs. It would be fairly safe to listen outside the kitchen door, she reckoned. If she was caught she could always pretend she had been on her way to the bathroom.

At first she could hear only her mother's voice, but it

38

was too low for her to make out any words and threads of panic began to tingle in her blood at the thought that her father might be too badly hurt to speak. Then her mother's voice became louder. It was half-scolding, half-imploring, and because she had heard the same things said before it was easy to make out the sense of them. *"You're not in the Belfast docks now, Patrick; you're in rural Scotland."* And, *"You'll never get the village to go against the gentry, Patrick."*

Still her father said nothing, but at the end of it she was surprised and pleased to hear him laugh. A minute later he called out loudly, as if her mother had gone into the scullery and he was shouting after her,

"God help them the day you stop Bible-thumping and take up politics. You'd make a grand orator, girl!"

Her mother called something back to him. She couldn't make out the sense of it, but whatever it was, it made her father laugh again.

"If I can't make Socialists," he shouted, "I can always breed 'em."

Another muffled reply from her mother, then her father's voice again,

"Bridie's the one with the gift of the gab. I'll convert her and sure as my name's Patrick McShane she'll make a better orator one day than both of us put together!"

There was a silence after that. She waited vainly for something else to happen but there was only the smell of cooking and the small sounds of her mother setting out a meal. Cautiously she began the journey back up

39

the stairs and was suddenly transfixed in a blaze of light from the open door of the kitchen.

Her father stood in the doorway. There was a bandage round his head and it was startlingly white against the brown of his skin. She froze, peering at him through the banisters, the bathroom excuse hunted from her brain by the suddenness of his appearance and the expression on his face. It was the face the Others were so afraid of, the stern face that was so seldom turned to her. She braced herself against the momentary spurt of fear it raised, till her usual determination to stand and fight against odds came to her aid.

"I came down to see if you got hurt at the meeting," she said.

"Is that an excuse, miss, or is it a reason?" he asked, and defiantly she threw back at him, "It's a reason."

He said nothing but moved closer till his face was only inches away from the other side of the banisters. Softly then, he asked,

"Bridie, who was Christ?"

Almost the parrotlike answer came tumbling off her tongue, but in the split second between thought and utterance she heard the echo of his voice, *"If I can't make Socialists I can always breed 'em."* Somewhere in her brain a connecting link snapped swiftly into place and triumphantly she answered, *"Christ was a revolutionary!"*

He smiled, the expression slowly broadening over his features till they were transformed into the great gleaming mask of mirth that so delighted her. "Sure?" he

40

asked. "Sure," she nodded. And grinning back at him she quoted the words of his boast. His chest heaved with silent mirth as she spoke and he whispered, "You're damn right I can, eh Bridie?"

For a moment longer they were held in the bond of secret, mutual laughter, then his hand reached through the banisters and pushed her gently upward.

"Hop it now, before your ma catches you," he whispered.

She hopped it, noiselessly scrambling up the remaining stairs. The closing kitchen door cut off the light from her before she reached the top, but with her father's sure hope of Heaven shining before her like a light she forgot her fear of the bogles that might be waiting to leap out on her. Quietly she got back into bed beside Moira, and lying there waiting for the warmth of the blankets to spread over her frozen limbs, she hugged to herself the inner warmth of the moment's conspiracy on the stairs.

The memory of her conversation with Mr. Gladsmuir recurred to her as she waited for sleep to come, and from the pinnacle of her new knowledge she looked down compassionately on the narrow bounds of the minister's views. Tomorrow, she thought, she would hunt through her Bible and find out exactly who Marx was. Tomorrow . . . that was the nicest thing about going to sleep— looking forward to tomorrow. Maybe Marx was one of the Old Testament prophets—Ezra, Nehemiah, Esther, Job . . . Silently she began to list the books of the

Old Testament but the tide of sleep rising in her brain washed the names away. She gave up, relying on the promise of tomorrow still ringing in her mind, and the lilt of the word was the last thing she remembered before sleep surged finally in on her that night.

4

The tomorrow she had looked forward to turned out to be a black day after all, for that was the day Mr. Muir split Mrs. Muir's head open with a hatchet. It was The War again, of course. Things like that kept happening in the street because of The War.

Ten o'clock in the morning Jessie Muir, the oldest daughter, came running up the path to their front door and burst into the kitchen. She was out in service with Lady Linton and only came home at weekends. And it was God's mercy she did, their mother said, or dear alone knows the slaughter there might have been among the other Muir bairns.

Jessie could hardly speak, her words were so mixed up with stammering and crying. Their father seized her by the shoulders and brought his hand, back and front, across her face. It was so swift and brutal that Bridie felt the crack and the shock of the slaps on her own flesh. She winced from it and from the scream that must surely come from Jessie; but she didn't scream, she only put

43

her hands up to her face and stared at him. Then she sighed, a long sobbing sigh and said quietly,

"It's my father, Mr. McShane. He's been desperate a' night wi' the pains in his feet. He started drinking and went for my mother wi' the hatchet when she tried to take the bottle from him."

Their father was at the cupboard taking out his first-aid box before she got that far.

"I got the ither bairns out of the house," Jessie went on, "and then I ran for you."

"Is she bad?"

"Gey bad. He split her head open wi' the first swing."

"Run for Bob Lees, lass," he told her. "Tell him to phone for the ambulance."

"The legs is gone from me," she said weakly. "I'll never make as far as the police station."

He took her by the shoulders again and pushed her to the door. "You'll have to, if you don't want your mother to die. Run, now! Run like the wind, girl!"

Nell said to their mother, "Can we go and look?"

She spoke very softly but their father caught the sound of it as he pushed the Muir girl out the door and spun round with a face of thunder on him.

"Stir out of this house," he roared, "and I'll have the hide off you! Isn't it bad enough the other bairns in this village are allowed to gawk at souls in torment without you behaving like vultures too?"

The storm of his voice filled the kitchen. They all shrank back from him, clutching at their mother's skirts.

44

Aileen got right behind her—she was always the timid one—and William clutched Bridie's hand with both of his. Their mother stretched her arms round them all like a hen spreading its wings over her chicks.

"I'll keep them in, Patrick," she said. "We'll pray for that poor man's soul."

"Aye, you do that," he said grimly, "and I'll go and bandage his wife."

As he disappeared out the door Moira said curiously, "How could Mr. Muir be desperate with the pain in his feet?"

Right enough, how could he? Bridie thought, and wondered why it hadn't occurred to her at the time. Mr. Muir had no feet. His legs had been cut off at the Battle of the Somme.

"It's just one of the things that happen with men wounded in The War," their mother told them. "They think they can still feel the pain in the limb even after it's been cut off. Now kneel down, children, and ask God's mercy for the terrible sin that poor man has taken on his soul."

It didn't make sense, Bridie thought, as she knelt obediently with William and the Others, and she felt a sneaking sympathy with Nell for daring to ask if they could go out and look. Maybe they'd have found out more about the pain that wasn't there if they had been allowed out. It wasn't fair. They always sent for her father when there was trouble in the street because he knew all about first aid and what to do with the police

45

and ambulance and all, and yet they were the only ones that didn't get to watch.

The other children had seen the body of the man that had hanged himself being carried out of the house, and they had seen her father lead Mr. Allison, weeping, into the ambulance, after he had slashed his wrists with a razor. She had heard them talking about it at school of course, but the only thing she had ever seen for herself was Mr. Souness going mad—and she wished she hadn't thought of that now because the pictures of it were coming back into her mind and she couldn't shut them out.

The men from the Council were mending a drain in the road, and she was hopping from one side to the other of the deep, chocolate-brown trench they had dug. Mr. Souness came out of his gate opposite the trench and began to walk along the street, and just then one of the men started up a pneumatic drill. Mr. Souness screamed when the noise started, the way the hares screamed at harvest-time when the boys hit them with sticks as they came running out of the last circle of uncut corn. He crouched down and put both hands over his head, and ran, crouching and screaming and clutching his head, away down the street. One of the workmen laughed and the ganger punched him on the nose and shouted, *"You'd laugh the other side of your bloody face if you had shell shock, mate!"* Then the drill was shut off and they all ran down the street after Mr. Souness.

They caught him and brought him back, but he was

still screaming and struggling to get away. Then she saw her father appearing at the other end of the street and she ran, shouting out to him. He ran towards her, and then past her, to the men trying to hold Mr. Souness down. He began to rap out orders, very quick and sharp, and presently the muddle around Mr. Souness was all straight again. Her father was kneeling down talking to him, and Mr. Souness was whimpering and holding on to her father's jacket with both hands.

She went inside then without waiting to be told to go. And later on, when her father came in and said, "Well, I hope you've prayed for poor Souness, Agnes. He's past all mortal help now," she had gone away upstairs and prayed for him herself—prayed really hard that he wouldn't always be horrible like that, squirming about on the ground and foaming at the mouth and whimpering.

Her mother was praying really hard for Mr. Muir's soul now. "Wrestling in prayer," they called it in the Brethren, and when her mother prayed like that it was easy to see why. She called on God so urgently to hear her that suddenly He seemed to be real and close, so close that the power and terror of His presence was pressing in all around them. The fast, powerful flow of her mother's words was going out to meet the power that was in God, and the argument between them swayed back and forth like a battle with her speaking for both of them—admitting and blaming, excusing and reminding, but all the time holding God to the promises of mercy He had made.

That was His weak spot and she kept driving in at it, reminding Him about there being more joy in Heaven over one sinner that repenteth and assuring Him she would see to it that Mr. Muir did repent. If only God would give her time, she pleaded, she would have him down on his knees crying, "God be merciful to me, a sinner."

But Mr. Muir had no knees, Bridie thought suddenly. How would he kneel? For that matter of it, how had he managed to balance himself for the blow that had split his wife's head with the axe? Had he just let himself fall forward on top of her, striking at her head as he went down?

Revolted, she turned away from the thought, but the fantastic picture of the legless cripple sprawled across the smashed head of his wife would not be blotted out of her mind. Nausea rose up in her throat. She jumped clumsily to her feet and rushed into the bathroom. The vomit rose vilely in her mouth as she reached the lavatory bowl, and when the retching finally stopped she collapsed weakly against it in miserable tears of self-pity.

Her head was spinning. She was only vaguely aware of her mother when she came in, but the arms raising her to her feet were comfortingly warm and solid. She pressed into her mother, wanting nothing more than the smell and the feel of her and the comfort of the small soothing sounds she made. But words broke from her, wrenched deep from some area of distress she did not know existed till she spoke,

"*Why* does there have to be wars, Mammy?"

"Ach now, my wee lamb, don't you worry your head over such terrible nonsense as wars. You're safe with Mammy now, see? Come on, my wee Bridie girl, come you and lie down . . ."

Her mother went on talking all the time she was taking her upstairs and putting a cold cloth on her forehead, and now she could feel a great tiredness overcoming her. She was tired, tired right down to the soles of her feet. Her very bones were tired. She wanted to sleep, sleep . . . you got away from everything when you slept . . . axe flashing down . . . screams . . . blood . . . head battered lying bloody, twisted sideways . . .

She began to cry, noisily now, holding on to her mother, trying to burrow into the warmth and softness of her again. Her mother rocked back and forward, holding her. The tears were hot in her throat, melting the hard painful lump that had gathered there and the gentle rocking soothed her. The crying eased down and the tiredness went with it, and when it was all over her mother laid her head gently back on the pillow and smoothed her brow. The palm of her hand was rough but the touch of it was cool and gentle.

When her mother went away she turned her head on the pillow and lay looking at the bright sunshine flickering off the leaves of the cherry tree outside the window. It was summer. Sunshine was summer, and summer was sunshine and swimming and playing on the beach and leaves very green. Gold and green summer was gold and green, very bright and shining. The colours flickering through the window reminded her how much she loved the summer. Gold and green were the colours of happiness. She *wanted* the summer to be happy. No more trouble in the street. It wasn't exciting, it was horrible—too horrible to think about. Don't think about it. Push it away—don't ask Dad any questions when he comes back. Green and gold, green and gold, pushed up in a big high barrier between her and the terrible things of The War. No more trouble in the street . . .

It worked, just as if she had made it work by thinking so hard about it. There was no more trouble in the street that year and gradually the fear of it slipped to the back of her mind. The school holidays were on and there were too many other things to think about.

That was the first summer she got to take William with her when she went down the sea-road carrying the basket with her father's tea in it. They always met halfway on the stretch of road it was his job to patrol, at the edge of the wood where the grass was short and thick on the road-verge and they could sit and look at the waves of the Firth rolling away—dark blue and slate blue near at hand, then grey tipped with white where they touched the coast of Fife on the opposite shore.

Her mother always put extra in the basket for her though it wasn't her proper teatime and sometimes, after the picnic-tea, her father taught her songs and they sang them together. He wasn't off duty, of course. He still had to jump up and salute cars that had the Association's badge on them, but she didn't mind that. In fact, she liked it. Her father was very smart in his uniform, standing up straight and saluting.

The grass at the picnic place was thick with daisies, and if she had to wait for him because he had been kept late by an accident or a breakdown, she passed the time making daisy chains for herself. She liked this. There was something fascinating about the neat splitting of each fleshy stalk with her thumbnail and the careful insertion into the split of the next stalk linking the long chain of flowers. She made daisy chains for William as well that summer.

William looked lovely wearing a daisy crown! His hair was very straight and fair, like her own. He had big grey eyes, and though he was a very solemn little boy, he had a way of suddenly laughing that made his eyes twinkle like her father's. Her father teased her about the daisy chains, but one day after she had made crowns and necklaces for herself and William and was working intently on a new chain, he came up so quietly to them that she didn't hear him. When she looked up he was standing staring at them with a very strange expression on his face. William laughed and held out his arms and her father gave a sound like a groan and went down on his knees and hugged them both.

She heard his heart beating thud-thud-thud in her ears and felt the roughness of his uniform tunic against her cheek. She gasped for breath, laughing and half-smothered in his embrace, and heard the muffled sounds of his own voice and William's, laughing and gasping as she was. He let them go and lay down beside them, leaning on one elbow and smiling at them.

"Sing now," he said. "Sing '*Paddy you're a villain*'."

So they sang together for him,

> *Paddy, you're a villain,*
> *Paddy, you're a rogue,*
> *There's nothin' o' ye Irish,*
> *Except yer name 'n brogue,*
> *Ye're killin' me by inches,*
> *Ye know I am yer slave,*
> *But when ye're dead, upon my soul—*
> *I'll dance upon yer grave!*

That was only one of the songs he had taught them. There was "Kelly, the Boy from Killarn" and "She moves through the Fair," and "The Soldiers' Song" and "Biddie Mulligan," and a lot of others. They were either very sad or very funny, her father's songs, and once when she asked him why this was, he said,

"It's because there is no one can weep so sore or laugh so hard as the Irish, my lass—but whether that's a gift or a curse, God alone knows."

And so that summer passed the way she had wanted it, with green and gold and singing. And then, in the autumn term when the school started again, he was ill.

5

Her mother told them about it when they came home from school the day he went into hospital.

"It's something to do with his War wounds," she said, "but it's not serious. Dr. McLaren says he won't be long in hospital."

But he was two months in hospital and that was the term she got into all the trouble at school.

It was the essays that did it, and being new in Miss Dunstan's class, and not being able to keep her temper. Miss Combe used to like her essays but Miss Dunstan didn't. She kept scoring things out in red pencil and changing the order of the words. Then she had to write it all out again the way Miss Dunstan wanted it and it looked different, not what she had wanted to write at all in the first place. And if she argued about it she got the belt, two strokes of the tawse on each hand. It hurt, but not so much as it hurt to see the words changed and, knowing the changes were wrong, still to lose the argument over the way the essay should be.

53

She hated Miss Dunstan. She hated the sleek dark bob of her hair, and the red lipstick that didn't match the red and orange dresses she wore. She hated her flying scarves and jangly bracelets. And more than anything she hated the twist of the thin lips and the sarcasm in the hard English voice reading her corrected essay aloud and ridiculing the words that had been scored out and changed.

She cried at home about her essays and her mother petted her and said, "Don't cry, my lamb." But she said, too, that she had to obey those set in authority over her; it was in the Scriptures that you had to. And her father wasn't there to tell.

She tried to imagine what he would have said. He had always told her that people should stand up for their rights. And it was her essay so surely she had a right to put it the way she wanted. It wasn't even as if the grammar or the punctuation was wrong. She was good at grammar. It was the order of the words and the kind of words she used that Miss Dunstan kept changing, and that changed the *feel* of the essay. And that belonged to her. Surely she had a right to put down the words the way she felt them?

She felt her temper rising and tried to control it. She had a terrible temper. Her mother said it was the Devil speaking through her, and that was true enough for only the Devil could cause the red rage that blazed through her sometimes. In school, on the next day that essays were due to be returned after marking, she held on to her temper, and when the green-covered jotters were handed out, opened hers slowly at the page where her latest essay had been written.

It was scored with red. The short, vivid marks patterned the pages so thickly that they looked like a crude, irregular design. "As if she had done it for fun!" she thought resentfully. She began to read over the essay and the red words Miss Dunstan had penciiled in beside each of the scored-out ones. It had been a homework essay—"A Description of the Sea," it was called—and they had been given a week to do it so she had taken time over it, lovingly choosing and picking among her pirate's treasure of words for the ones that had the right sound and colour about them, carefully fitting them together like a mosaic in one pencilled draft after another till the final pattern had been achieved.

It had been a wonderful feeling when it was finished. But now she was staring at the ruin of her lovely pattern of words, and though the rage was rising redly in her brain she didn't care a damn—she didn't care a bloody damn for Miss Dunstan and her belt. She looked up and straight into Miss Dunstan's eyes.

"As you can see, Bridget," Miss Dunstan said, "you will have to rewrite your essay *again*. Why you persist in using these ridiculous turns of phrase—"

She interrupted her, shouting across the cold barrier of reproof. "*I don't give a bloody damn for you and your belt!*"

"Come out! Come out here!" Miss Dunstan's face was

all bones and hollows with her own rage. The tears spurted out of Bridie's eyes and with horror she saw a look of satisfaction cross Miss Dunstan's face. She thought she was crying because she was going to get the belt again—but she wasn't, she wasn't crying for that!

She tried to explain, fighting to control her breath. "It's all wrong—you've made it all wrong. The words don't fit any more. You've broken the picture, it's not—"

"That's enough!" The belt was swishing back over Miss Dunstan's shoulder. It flicked the neat black bob of her hair making it fly out wildly round the wild, strained look on her face. "I've put up with enough from you, you—you little Irish bog-trotter!"

The words themselves meant nothing to Bridie. The insult they held was clear enough. She glared, speechless, unable with the paralysis of rage that gripped her to hold out her hand even if she had willed it.

"If Mahomet won't come to the mountain," Miss Dunstan said between her teeth, "then the mountain shall come to Mahomet."

She took two swift strides forward and lashed downwards. The belt whipped round the calves of Bridie's bare legs. It was the short belt of heavy leather, the "tawse" used in all Scottish schools, and the pain of the blow was intense.

Involuntarily she cried out. The fiery stroke of the belt whipped round her legs again. She staggered under the impact crying out again at the pain, and above the sound of her own voice heard the banging of the class-room door and the voice of Mrs. Mackie, the headmistress, calling Miss Dunstan's name.

"Go back to your seat, Bridie," Mrs. Mackie said.

She went back to her seat, too shocked by the sudden onslaught and the pain to be able to think. There was nothing in her mind now except a vague wonder and fear of what had happened. Mrs. Mackie spoke quietly to Miss Dunstan for a few minutes, then she picked up Bridie's jotter and looked at it, studying the scored pages. Still looking at it, she read out,

"And waves like green broken glass fell jaggedly down."

She looked up. "That is what you wrote, Bridie," she said quietly. "I see that the phrase 'green broken glass' has been changed to read, 'broken green glass.' Is there any difference? And if so, can you tell me where it lies?"

She could see it all right, but it was hard to explain. She tried, haltingly. "Broken green glass—it's just ordinary, just what it says. 'Broken green glass.' A bottle, a dish, anything ordinary."

"Go on." Mrs. Mackie's face was not encouraging but her voice was still soft.

"Well, the other way," she tried again, "it's *not* ordinary any more because the sound has a sort of pattern to it. You know—like the notes of a song, rising and falling. And changing the order of the words to 'green broken glass'—well, it makes them look different, mysterious all of a sudden . . ."

57

Her voice faltered, trailing away under Mrs. Mackie's look, and almost in a whisper she finished, ". . . as if they had a sort of magic about them . . ."

And then, because she had managed at last to explain something of the feeling that had been in her mind when she wrote her essay, she realized suddenly how much she needed adult reassurance that she was right. Pleadingly, before Mrs. Mackie could speak, she asked,

"Do *you* not think so, miss?"

Mrs. Mackie said drily, "I think you may have glimpsed the shadow of the edge of the meaning of poetry, Bridie." She turned back to Miss Dunstan and spoke to her again. Miss Dunstan went very red in the face but she said nothing, then Mrs. Mackie handed Bridie back her jotter.

"Bridie," she said very seriously, "we will forget today's disgraceful scene on condition that you submit to Miss Dunstan's discipline in future. That means accepting any corrections that are made in your essays. You understand?"

She nodded and managed a whisper of "Yes, miss," but her heart was bitter for she had begun to think Mrs. Mackie was on *her* side.

"Good girl," Mrs. Mackie said briskly. "You will be in my class next year, Bridie, and I can promise you that *I* will look forward to essays with 'a sort of magic' in them."

She smiled, then she was gone and the class was

whispering and Miss Dunstan was writing on the black-board and it was all over. Except for that smile—wonderful, like the sun coming out! And the promise about next year!

Her heart singing in her now, Bridie lifted the lid of her desk, pretending to be looking in it for something so that her expression was hidden from Miss Dunstan. She still didn't give a bloody damn for her and her old belt, she thought exultantly. *And* she had stood up for her rights. Her father would be pleased about that!

She told him about it when he came out of hospital two weeks later, though she knew she would be punished for the swearing part of it. She was, too. Early to bed every night that week and no Sunday walk with him and William. But he was angrier with Miss Dunstan than he was with her. She knew that and she wondered what he would do about it.

When he came down to meet her coming out of school the next day she guessed what was in the wind. She waited where he told her to, outside Mrs. Mackie's study, but though she strained her ears she couldn't hear what was being said while he was in there. It was only when he opened the door slightly as he was leaving that she heard anything of the conversation. First it was Mrs. Mackie's voice at the tail end of a sentence.

". . . and certainly has an unusual grasp of language for her age, though she will undoubtedly have to discipline that temper of hers."

Her father laughed. "It's the old rebel in her," he

said, pulling the door towards him. "She's Irish as a bog, that one."

The door opened wider and she darted away to stand demurely by the entrance into the playground. Her father stood in the study doorway, smiling and shaking hands with Mrs. Mackie, then he joined her and they walked away out of the school together.

He was very thoughtful going up the road, looking at the ground, hands in his pockets and whistling through his teeth. At the big oak tree—the one where, they were taught at History, George Wishart had preached and John Knox had carried the sword for him —he stopped and looked thoughtfully down at her.

"It seems," he said at length, "that Aileen's not the only one in the family worthy of a higher education. I gather that you must have been there too, when the brains were handed out."

He paused and swayed back on his heels, looking up into the great spread of the oak's branches as if the words he was looking for could be found hiding under the canopy of the leaves, and after a while he said, still looking up,

"The dear alone knows how I'll manage it for the both of you, but as I'm a living Irishman, if you're worth a good education, Bridie, you shall have it."

His gaze swept down to her. "D'ye hear me?"

"Yes, Dad," she said obediently, and because it was the only thing that was important to her then, she asked immediately, "Does that mean I'll get to write what I want?"

The smile, his wonderful smile, began to ripple over his face and his eyes fairly danced at her. "Bridie," he said, "oh, Bridie! If you could only see yourself standing there! You're only the size of tuppence, but your chin's stuck out like a prizefighter's in a ring and I wouldn't give a tinker's cuss for *anyone* that tried to stop you doing what you want to do!"

"Ach, Dad, don't laugh at me," she protested. "There's nothing wrong with liking words, is there?"

"Nothing at all," he said. "Nothing at all. Learn enough of them and you might even write a book one day."

She burst out laughing at that but he put his hand on her shoulder as they walked on and said quite seriously, "Think about it, Bridie. Think about it. If you have a gift you should cultivate it early." And farther up the road he said, "As for the temper, my girl, there's not much I can say about that for I'm the one you've taken it off, and I doubt if there's an Irishman born that can keep his temper when he's provoked. You'll just have to try, that's all, and take an example off your mother for there never was a gentler woman than her."

She did try, of course, but it didn't do much good, her rage came up so quickly it was on her before she knew. As for the idea of writing a book, she didn't think of that again till they were really into winter and it was

dark by the time she got home from school in the after-
noons. They couldn't go out to play at nights then, and
when she was looking around for something to do she
remembered about the book. The trouble was, what was
the book to be about?

She puzzled about it and puzzled about it, then one
day she came on the packet of letters and knew that her
problem was solved.

6

The letters were in a wooden box on the top shelf of the little carved cupboard that hung on the wall of the back bedroom. All the family papers were kept in this cupboard along with ink and writing materials, and so it was the first place she looked in that day for writing paper to start her book.

The shelf on which the box lay was above her head. She pushed up the lid of it, felt inside, touched paper, and tried to pull the box gently down. It slid too quickly off the shelf and she caught it as it toppled. A folded sheet of writing paper fell out. It was closely written on in her mother's neat hand and she put it quickly back in the box, but as she closed the lid on it the meaning of the opening sentence stared up at her from the paper.

"Dear Mr. McShane,
    "I have been asked by the Red Cross to 'adopt' a soldier from their list of Prisoners of War . . ."

The opening of the second letter in the pile confirmed

her guess at the contents of the box. It was in her father's copperplate writing and it started,

"Dear Miss Armstrong,
   "Your letter came as a great surprise to me and I was deeply moved by the kindness of its tone . . ."

She had put the box down on the floor so that she could replace the first letter and take the second one out without fear of spilling the other letters it contained, and now she knelt beside it with a great struggle going on in her mind.

She knew the story of how her father and her mother had first become acquainted. Dad had been wounded and captured in The War, and Miss Hall, the Red Cross lady, had asked Mam to write to one of the men in his camp, and Mam had picked his name off the list because he had been the only Dublin Fusilier in that camp and she thought he would be lonelier than the other men who had pals from their own regiments to talk to. So they wrote to one another, often and often. Then they fell in love with one another and he asked her to marry him without their even having seen one another. Grandpa had been very angry but after a while he liked Dad too and so they got married after all.

That was all she knew, but she had so often wanted to know more about it and now here were the very letters they had written. Dare she read them? Nobody would ever know—except God, of course. He was always watching and it would be a sin, a terrible, terrible sin.

Her hand crept out to the box. It would be her last sin, after all, even if it was a big one. After this she was determined to be good. And in any case, she had more than sixty of her three-score years and ten left to do good deeds in to make up for the sin before God got her. She began to read.

Her father's letters were easier to read than those in her mother's small, spiky handwriting and it puzzled her when he apologized in the first one for his writing.

"The Army gave me the first schooling I ever had," he wrote, "and it may be that the foolish loyalty I have to the childish style of hand they taught me has its roots in the gratitude I have always felt for the world of books their schooling enabled me to discover."

The letters were short at first and full of little phrases like the ones in her mother's *"Book of Etiquette and Table Manners"*—"I trust your health is improving . . . I send you my kind regards . . ." and things like that. Then came one letter that, instead of starting, "Dear Miss Armstrong," began,

"Dear Agnes,
"Please allow me to call you so—'dear Agnes,' because your letters, so eagerly awaited, such joy to read, have made you very dear to me. Not only, believe me, because I am a lonely man and a prisoner in a

strange land, but because there is a goodness and
sweetness about them that shows the tender warmth
of your nature better than any description of yourself
could do. And if, from that goodness of heart, you can
bring yourself to write to me as 'dear Patrick,' I shall
count myself as a man with a view of heaven rather
than the tangled prospect of barbed wire that faces me
now . . ."

She gave a little sigh of delight when she read this
and for a moment laid the letter down on her knees. "A
man with a view of heaven,"—oh, it was a fine phrase,
a bobby-dazzler of a phrase! He must be a poet born,
her father!

He got his "dear Patrick" too, but for a while he didn't
get beyond that except for a shy, "Your dear friend,
Agnes," at the foot of a letter instead of the "Your sin-
cere friend," that had finished the earlier ones.

She read on, eagerly searching for the signs of friend-
ship passing into the falling-in-love stage she had heard
about. Her mother's letters were mostly about things at
home in Edinburgh; working with Grandpa in his shop,
rolling bandages for the Red Cross, singing hymns with
the Brethren's choir to the soldier-patients in hospital,
thinking out ways to meet the problems that arose from
the shortage of food. About this she wrote,

"We must all, Mother and my sisters and I, now
learn to do without sugar, for my brother, Tom, is so
fond of sweet things that he cannot do without, and

66

Mother says we must make the sacrifice for him as he is
soon to be a soldier and needs the nourishment."

Rotten greedy pig, she thought indignantly, and the
next moment was giggling as she read,

"I am, I fear, in great disgrace for laughing in the
meeting on Sunday past, but the truth is that Brother
Harris, who was expounding the Word, has a voice so
like a sheep bleating that I could not resist the
temptation to laugh, which excited the girls beside me
to the point where they laughed too. The Devil
tempted me again at this, and I bleated aloud in
mockery of Brother Harris—very softly, but still I
bleated, and Father ordered me to leave the meeting.

"Afterwards he said to me, 'Brother Harris has the
brain as well as the voice of a sheep—I am well aware
of that—but it is still not fitting to proclaim the fact
aloud in the House of God.' However, the giggles were
still on me which made Father really angry and I was
confined to my room for the rest of the day. From
which you will see, Patrick, that I am very prone to
laughter—indeed, I am afraid Father is right when he
says it is my besetting sin."

There were quite a number of funny stories like this
in her mother's letters and her father seemed to like
reading them, but his letters were much more serious.
Perhaps because of the pain. He had a lot of pain it
seemed, from his wounds, and there was no proper hospital in the camp. She tried to pin down the nature of

his wounds but the words he used were beyond her understanding, and she puzzled, too, over the letters where he spoke of another pain.

"There is no physical pain," he wrote, "to compare with the mental suffering a man undergoes when he takes stock of himself and his kind. Here, God-endowed, we live like beasts in a fog of despair and hatred. All our intellects have achieved nothing more than this terrible end—that men should wantonly smash the beautiful mechanism of other men's bodies into useless hulks of flesh, and prison one another in cages far more impenetrable than those used for the fiercest of animals.

"I have taken stock, and I know now that we are all, German and British alike, prisoned and maimed. For before the guns began, hatred had done its work, and before the bars were put up the lack of understanding of which we are all guilty had imprisoned us."

But it was in this letter too, that she came on a sentence which threw light on many things that had puzzled her before, for later on in it he wrote,

"You say we are all God's children, and I feel that all men should be brothers. In essence, we are saying the same thing. Let us continue to hold it before us for it is the only thing that can light us through the dark world men have created from their own evil; it is the only glimpse we shall ever have of the little spark of the divine in man."

68

The confused memory of a thousand arguments filled her head. Her father's voice saying, *"Christianity versus Socialism—come on, Agnes, marshal your facts!"* and then their voices rising and falling, her mother's fervent and vibrating with feeling, her father's measured, precise, but rolling with urgency like a strong river held in check. The teasing, the laughter that followed, and the looks passing between them that she had never understood before. This was the beginning of it—these letters. Here was the reason for the deep cleavage she had always sensed between them, and here too, was the first span of the strong bridge they had thrown across the chasm.

She sat lost in thought. It took a long time to sort it out in her mind, and when it had settled into a pattern of meaning she turned eagerly back to the letters. The next one was from her mother, and it was this one that burst through the last cautious barrier between the two of them. It was a short letter, but it contained enough to horrify her.

"This morning the Casualty Lists came out and Father was given one to post up in the shop. Oh, Patrick, it was dreadful! So many of the Dandy Ninth —Edinburgh's own regiment—have been killed. So many beautiful boys all dead! I went to school with them, we grew up together, and worst of all, I know their mothers and their sisters and their wives. All morning they have been crowding into the shop. The

69

news-stands are sold out and there are only the publicly posted lists, such as ours, to search. The cries and the screams—my mind will never be rid of them! Father prayed aloud to try and comfort the women, but it was no use. He could not be heard above the crying and his anguish for them was terrible to witness. I never thought to see my own father in tears.

"By midday we could endure it no longer. Father closed the shop and nailed the list to the door and we all went home. He and the rest of the family are praying now in his study but I cannot bear to be with them. I had to write to you, wicked and wrong as it is to be thinking of myself at such a time. I need the comfort of your words to carry me through this darkness. I feel so alone. How is it possible to feel so alone when my family is all around me? And yet I do, except when I am writing to you or reading one of your letters. Write to me. Write quickly, for I find the loneliness hard to bear."

And then came the reply—"*My own beloved girl*—" and a letter of such tenderness that she felt hot tears prickling under her eyelids. She dropped the letter and covered her face with her hands, and shame swept over her with unbearable force. It had not been a sin to read the letters—it was something far, far worse than that for even God had no right to read this beautiful letter. No one but her mother had any right to read it—no one at all.

In an agony of remorse she rocked back and forward on her knees, desperately trying to put a name to the thing she had done, too lost in the depths of her shame and bewilderment to hear the door opening or to realize her mother's presence in the room. It was only when her mother spoke sharply to her that she came back to her surroundings, with her heart giving a great jump of terror on the sound. And though her mother had never struck a blow in anger at her in all her life, she flinched and cowered away from her.

There was no blow, no more sound from her mother. She looked up, and blinking at the tears coming so fast now that they blinded her said chokingly,

"I'm sorry, Mam. I'm awful sorry. I found them and I —I wanted to know about you and Dad falling in love. I'm awful sorry, Mam."

Her mother bent down and picked up the last letter, the one she had dropped.

"You read this?"

She nodded miserably. "That was when I knew I shouldn't—I mean—oh Mam, I don't *know* what I mean, but I shouldn't have! I'm sorry, I'm sorry!"

She couldn't stop crying now. It was coming out of her in great gulps and sobs and her nose was all choked up and her chest hurt.

"Ssh, Bridie. Ssh, child, you'll make yourself ill."

Her mother gathered the letters quickly together and put them in the box, then knelt down beside her and hugged her tight. "I'm not angry with you, dearie. Not now you know it was wrong and are sorry."

"Truly not angry?"

71

"Truly. God forgives us when we're sorry, doesn't he? Well, I'd be a poor Mammy to you if *I* couldn't forgive you, eh?"

Bridie clung to her. Her heart was bursting with love for her mother but she could find nothing to say but, "Oh, Mammy!"

"I know, I know," her mother said, and a great peace descended on her. Her mother did know. There *were* no words for love like this.

Her sobs trailed off into sniffles and then the sniffles stopped too and there was nothing but the silence and the peace of her mother holding her. Into the quietness, her mother said softly.

"Will I tell you the end of the story?"

Drowsily she answered, "Yes, please," and her mother said,

"I never thought to tell it to any of you before. But you're girls, after all—you'll have problems too, maybe . . ."

She stopped, without finishing the sentence. Bridie waited, and after a few moments her mother began to speak again.

"I was twenty-five when your father wrote that letter asking me to marry him," her mother said. "Old enough, as I thought, to know my own mind. But my father thought differently. I was old enough to run the shop and do all his accounts for him—indeed, he always said I had a better business head than any of your uncles—but not old enough to decide who I was going

72

to marry. I had to ask his permission, of course, before I could write and say 'yes' to your father, but when I spoke to him about it both he and Mother were horrified.

" 'Marry a man you've never met!' they said—oh, and a lot more besides.

" 'He's Irish!' they said, the same way they might have said, 'He's a leper!'

"Of course they were thinking that meant he was a Roman Catholic, and when I quoted his own saying, 'Human-kind is my religion,' Father nearly had a fit. And Mother said, 'He's got no money, no job to come back to after The War.' And they both asked, 'Who are his parents? What's his trade? Is he respectable?' And, of course, I couldn't answer a thing. All I knew about him was from his letters and from these."

She leaned forward, took two photographs from under the pile of letters in the box, and held them in front of her. Bridie stared at them. They were both of her father in soldier's uniform but one was a studio portrait and the other was a snapshot and the difference between them was such that at first she thought they must be photographs of two different men.

The face in the studio portrait was a handsome one of a young man with thick, fair hair, a straight, delicate-boned nose, and a firm mouth humorously set. His eyes stared back at her, deep-set, but clear and friendly, with more than the hint of a twinkle in them.

The snapshot showed him standing against an untidy background of wooden huts and barbed wire. The immaculate uniform of the first photograph was crumpled and shabby and he was leaning heavily on a stick; but it was in the face that the real difference between the photographs lay. In the second photograph the firm mouth had thinned to a grim line of endurance. The smoothness of his face had become deeply indented with lines running downwards from nose to mouth. His hair had thinned, showing a bald patch on his scalp at the front, and the twinkle in the eyes that looked into hers had been replaced by a fierce and terrible sadness.

"The first one was taken at the beginning of The War," her mother told her. "The other one—the one in the prison camp—was taken after he had been there for two years without any proper treatment for his wounds. He sent them both to me when he wrote that letter."

Bridie nodded, remembering the words she had just read,

> "You will see from the photographs how little my attractions are for I do not even have my health left to offer you. I have nothing except the hope that I may have kindled in your heart a little flame of the great fire of love that burns in mine."

Looking from one photograph to the other and remembering what he had written, a feeling she could not understand stirred in her. It was anger, or it was love, or it was a mixture of both; she could not tell. But from it, the words rushed out,

"Grandpa was wrong—he was wrong, Mam. I mean, all the things he thought were important, they weren't really, were they?"

"Not important at all," her mother said quietly. "They said I didn't know him and in the sense they meant it, that was true—"

"But you knew—" Bridie interrupted, and stopped, knowing what she wanted to say but with no words at her command to express it. Her mother supplied them.

"Yes, I knew his soul. And I loved him for it, loved him enough to go against my parents' orders and write to tell him that I *would* marry him."

There was a little silence as she placed the photographs carefully back in the box, then she said,

"You have to understand, Bridie, that, even though I was sure I loved him, that was a big step to take. Nowadays, you hear even small children speaking back to their parents, but in those days, and even at the age I was then, it was a terrible thing for me to defy my father. When I told him what I had done he was angrier than I had ever seen him. He's a kind man, your Grandpa, you know that, Bridie. And he's a good man that rarely gives way to anger. But he told me then that God would never forgive the sin I had committed."

"Yes, He would," Bridie told her confidently. " 'God is Love'—it's up there on the big text."

75

She pointed to the big, framed text hanging on the wall and her mother laughed and hugged her.

"You've got a funny little mind," she said through the laughter, "but I think I can see what you're driving at. God would understand it was because I loved him—is that it?"

Yes, that was it, Bridie told her, and impatiently leaping ahead to the conclusion of the story, asked,

"But how could you marry him while he was still a prisoner?"

"He was sent to a London hospital six months later on a Red Cross exchange of seriously wounded Prisoners of War," her mother said. "Miss Hall, the Red Cross lady, came to tell me about it and I asked Father's permission to go to visit him at the hospital. Well, he refused his permission, but I was determined to go all the same. The trouble was, I had no money for the fare. I got my board and keep for working in the shop but all I had for myself was a few shillings in pocket money. So I decided to raise the fare by selling my new bicycle.

"I didn't dare to do it myself in case Father heard about it, so I got Jack Menteith to do it for me—he was one of the Menteith family that used to live next door to us; I've told you about them, remember? A nice boy, Jack, and he'd been sweet on me ever since we went to school together, so I knew I could trust him not to say a word."

She smiled, remembering, and went on, "I slipped off that Saturday night with the fare in my pocket and got on the London train—and my, I was scared! I'd never been as far from home as London in my life before and I didn't know a soul there. And I was scared of what I was doing, too—going to meet a man I'd never seen and defying my father to do it! I was so keyed up that when the train whistle went off suddenly as we drew out of the station I nearly fainted with the fright I got.

"That part of it was bad enough, but it was worse walking down the hospital ward to meet your father. It was a great long ward and he was in a bed at the farthest end of it. The Sister walked ahead of me to show me his bed, and I think I'll remember till my dying day the look of her back. I didn't dare to glance aside at the men in the beds we passed, and all I could see was the back of her blue frock with the broad white straps of her apron crossed over it. Then she stopped, and I stopped, and she said,

" 'Mr. McShane, I've brought you a visitor.'

"Then she stepped aside and I saw your father for the first time."

"What did he say?" Bridie whispered.

"He didn't say a thing," her mother said, "and neither did I. He was sitting up in bed with his hands lying clenched on the sheet on either side of him. We just looked at one another, and then he smiled—you know that smile of his, Bridie. He brought his right hand up and I saw that he was holding a ring in it. I went forward to him and he took my left hand and slipped the ring on my engagement finger."

77

She stopped at that point and after a moment began to rise to her feet, taking the box of letters with her. Putting it back in the cupboard she said,

"It took Father a long time to calm down when I came home wearing that ring, but I wasn't worried about that. I knew he'd come round to Patrick once he'd met him—everyone does! Your father could charm a bird off its nest the way he talks, and when he came to Edinburgh after the hospital had discharged him he soon had Father in the hollow of his hand. Mother too."

She laughed, turning her head to look down on Bridie. "I remember Mother said she hadn't met such a mannerly man since her own young days. No, there was no more trouble about us getting married after that."

She smiled again, and the happiness in her face made it so beautiful all of a sudden that Bridie did something she hadn't done since she was little. She flung her arms round her mother, and with one cheek pressed against her she rocked from side to side, from one foot to the other, softly chanting,

"*Mammy, mammy, mammy! Mammy, mammy, mammy!*"

Her mother's arms came round her as her body yielded to the rocking motion, and she murmured in return the low, loving sound that went with the chant from the baby days.

"I was going to write a book," Bridie said, suddenly

freeing herself. "You know that? I was going to write a book and I found the box when I was looking for paper to write on. It was Dad who said I should write a book."

"Well, maybe you can. You could try anyway," her mother said. "Here—" she turned to the cupboard again, took some paper out and handed it to her, "—there's the paper you were looking for. But what's the book to be about? Fairies? Pirates?"

"No," she said slowly. "No." The great idea was being born and she was feeling it taking shape in her mind. Still speaking very slowly she said,

"It'll be about you—and Dad—and The War—and all that, you know, about the letters and you getting married—and Grandpa being so horrible—"

"Ach, your poor old Grandpa, he's not a villain!" Her mother was laughing, pushing her gently ahead of her to the door of the bedroom. "I'm afraid you'll not make much of a story out of all that, my lamb."

"I will, too!"

She was quite confident about it for already the words and ideas were bubbling up in her brain. As they went downstairs she asked,

"What was Dad before he joined the Army?"

"He wasn't anything," her mother said sadly. "He didn't have the chance. He was only a little thing when his mother died and his father married again. His stepmother gave him an awful time of it till he ran away and joined the Army as a drummer boy."

"A drummer boy!" she echoed, and with a sigh of

79

delight felt the first sentence of her book forming from the fine, romantic ring of the word.

"One night, a terrible night of wind and rain it was, a poor ragged boy came knocking at the captain's door and asked to join the Army . . ."

Her mind leaped ahead of the scene with the desperate waif driven out into the stormy night. A day of bright sunshine grew in its place with a column of brightly coloured soldiers marching through it, and at its head, a drummer boy in blue and scarlet (with silver braid?) and white drumsticks flashing the beat up and down on the drum bobbing in front of him.

The rest of what was said, if anything else was said as they went downstairs, fell on deaf ears. She was well launched on the drummer boy's career now. He had become a sergeant with a sleeveful of stripes and he was going off to fight in the Great World War.

Without any true realization of how she had got there she found herself sitting at the table by the kitchen window, with her pencil travelling over the smooth white face of the paper in front of her. Everything around her had gone dead. The clock on the kitchen mantelpiece had stopped ticking. The voices of William and the Others scrabbling over some game on the floor had vanished along with the furnishings of the room. She was alone in a new, strange world with the drummer boy and the captain and the sergeant and trainloads of soldiers and the Red Cross lady and a beautiful woman writing letters . . .

It was a shock, when she had to move aside for the table being set for tea, to come back to the real world. She was too dazed at first to cover up what she had been doing and the title page of the book lay open to Nell's curious gaze—"*The Man with a View of Heaven*" by Bridie McShane."

"That's a funny name for an essay," Nell said, and in a burst of pride she retorted,

"It's not an essay, it's a book. I'm writing a book."

Immediately Moira and Aileen were beside Nell at the table and teasing was flying at her like a storm of hailstones. She defended herself loudly against the jeers, but it was three to one with William looking solemnly on and not old enough to help her. They were shouting her down when a word she had heard the previous day came to her aid, a word that would make the whole situation gloriously clear, and triumphantly she shouted above their din,

"I can too write a book, see! Because I'm going to be an *authoress!*"

Gleefully they pounced on the word, throwing it from one to the other, twisting the sound of it till they had a malicious chant of "Author-*ass!* Author-*ass!*" dinning at her, and with shame she realized the trap of ridicule she had sprung on herself. She was always being caught like this. The trap was always there, baited with her delight in airing a new word, but it was only after the word was out that she realized she had blundered into it again.

She had tried to make them see that the delight was for the words alone, for the sound and the feel of them and the marvellous way they allowed her to unlock ideas from her mind, but they wouldn't believe her. They thought she was just showing off and the mockery was their way of punishing her.

"Bridie's swallowed the dictionary! Bridie's swallowed the dictionary!"

Nell began the taunting chant that followed her in the playground when she had blundered into the trap at school and the other two joined in with her. Her mother called to them from the scullery where she was making the tea but they paid no attention and it was only her father's entrance that stopped the tormenting voices in the end. Even he smiled, however, when they told him what all the laughing and shouting was about. He grinned at her and ruffled her hair with his hand.

"Remember us," he said, "when you're rich and famous."

She jerked her head away from under his hand. She had laughed herself, to begin with, at the idea that she should write a book, but now that she had actually started it there was nothing funny about it. *He* should see that—it had been his idea in the first place, and resentfully including him in the thought she told herself that if ever she did become a rich and famous authoress they would all be sorry for making a fool of her, and serve them right. She had sense enough to keep the thought to herself, however, and after that she only worked on her book in secret in the box-room at the top of the stairs.

It made a fine hiding place, the box-room. There was no light there but she stole a candle for it from the scullery cupboard. The barricade of trunks she built across the middle of the box-room floor made sure that no tell-tale line of light showed under the door, and whenever she could slip away from the kitchen unobserved she worked at her book behind the barricade.

It was a curious feeling to be so secret and alone while the life in the rest of the house went on without her. For the first few minutes each time she went into the box-room she could have cried with the terrible feeling of loneliness it gave her. Then the attraction that had drawn her there would take hold. All the people who had grown somehow in her mind would take shape again from the shadows and she would see them, first, frozen in various poses like the people on the slides at the Magic Lantern Lectures the Literary Society gave in the church hall. Then the frozen pictures would move, and she would hear them talk as they grew into people so warm and real that it seemed to her it was she who had become the shadowy one listening and watching unseen from her candle-lit corner.

Once, when her father had taken her to a theatre in Edinburgh to see a great actor because, he said, he's an old man now and you may never see him again but you can always tell your children you saw him, he had pointed out to her a little, lit box in front of the stage and told her there was a man called "the prompter" hidden there. He had a copy of the play in his hand so that he could remind the actors what to say if they forgot their words, and it seemed to her that something like this was happening in the box-room. She was hidden like the prompter and her people were acting out a story like the actors she had seen on the stage. The difference was that the copy she had was being written out while the play went on, and it was not she who prompted the actors. When she was stuck for a word, they prompted her.

They were her secret all that winter. She grew to love them with such a fierce and jealous love that the lightest touch of ridicule on them—even a smile and a joke from her father like the one he had made when the Others told him she was writing a book—would have spoiled the secret pleasure they gave her. And yet, it was the first time apart from things like where his birthday present was hidden that she had ever had a secret from him. The knowledge shamed her and she began to cast around in her mind for a way of making up to him for her deceitfulness—some way that wouldn't involve telling anyone about the book.

7

That winter, the winter of her book, was the terrible hard one when they had all the frost and snow. The hard weather was bad for her father. His face began to have a pinched, grey look and the lines on it became deeper. Her mother worried about him being out all day in the icy cold, but he wouldn't listen to her.

"I'm lucky to have a job at all, with my disability," he told her. "Just thank your lucky stars we're not like these thousands of poor devils trying to exist on the dole."

The lanes to the outlying farms were filled from dike to dike with snow that winter, and every day the children from Redmains and Castlebrae arrived at school with their boots soaked and the littlest ones crying with the cold. The wet boots and socks were put to dry round the stove in the infants' room and Miss Scott, the infant mistress, made tea for the farm children to heat their insides. That stopped the little ones crying because it was fun sitting round the stove in bare feet and drink-

85

ing tea. But when school was over they started crying again because the leather of their boots was all cracked and hard with the heat of the stove and it hurt to put them on again.

Her father was furious when he heard about the farm children. Her mother tried to calm him but he went on shouting till she said, quite angrily for her,

"But what can you *do* about it, Patrick?"

"I can raise enough hell to get those so-called landed gentry on the County Council off their backsides and doing something about clearing the lanes for a start!" he roared. "They can't blacklist me, you know. I'm not one of their serfs that daren't join a union in case he gets the sack and has to say, 'Yes sir, no sir, three bags full, sir,' every time the laird opens his mouth."

They were all afraid of him when he was as angry as this. Even her mother was frightened as a rule, but this time she stood up to him.

"There's gentry on the Board that employs you too," she said. "They're all Captain This and the Honourable That and they're all hand in glove with the gentry on the Council. You've crossed that lot enough, Patrick. I'm telling you, they're only waiting for an excuse now to put you out of a job. Then where will *we* be—myself and the bairns?"

Her father had sat down to unlace his boots while she spoke. Now he looked up at her mother and his face was hard and still as brown stone. He turned his head and looked round at them all watching him, then he said quietly,

"Yes. I have given hostages."

He got to his feet. "Patrick—" her mother began, but he interrupted her. "I shouldn't have married you," he said. "I shouldn't have married anyone."

The bitterness in his voice was terrible to hear, and for the second that he stood there after he had spoken, Bridie felt herself touched chillingly by a sense of the loneliness that was in him. Then he brushed past her mother and went out of the kitchen.

William asked, as he always did every time their father went out, "When's my daddy comin' *back*?" but her mother hushed him down and said quickly to them all,

"You're not to judge your father by things like this. He's a good man. It's just his quick temper makes him say things he doesn't mean."

Bridie opened her mouth to protest. Her father hadn't been in a rage when he made that strange remark about hostages. He had meant what he said. A warning look from her mother silenced the argument on her lips, but later that day when her mother called her to go a message to the grocer's, she brought the subject up again.

"You see too much, Bridie," she said, "far more than you should for your age. But some day you'll have children of your own and then, maybe, you'll spare a little

87

of the pity you had for your father for me instead."

Obediently she said, "Yes, Mam," and escaped as quickly as she could, for it made her uncomfortable to hear her mother talking with that little break in her voice that sounded as if she might begin to cry. Going down the street with the message-basket she thought that winter wasn't the fun it was made out to be in books, and wondered why story-children seemed to enjoy it so much more than real children. They played the same winter games as story-children, after all, but snowballing wasn't any fun because the big boys put lumps of ice in their snowballs. Sledging was no use either because their shoes got wet and then they had to come indoors till they dried because they only had the one pair each. And with the terrible price shoes were, they didn't dare to slide much either for fear of sliding holes in the soles of their shoes.

There was never anything in the books, for that matter of it, about the birds they kept finding dead in the snow, feathers all damp and fragile legs sticking so pitifully stiff from their little bodies. And what about the horses? There was nothing in the books about the terror the winter held for the big, clumsy cart horses when the roads were too icy to give their hooves a grip. It was awful to see the way they laboured, slipping and sliding up the steep brae of the village street with the terror of falling rolling wildly round in their eyes.

"What happens—what *happens* if one them falls?" she had asked anxiously of a carter one day, falling into step with him as he walked beside his cart.

"Och, we have to shoot the poor beast, lassie," he told her. "They heavy yins are near certain to break a leg when they fa', and then there's nothing we can dae but put a gun tae its heid."

It was worse, much worse after that, watching the horses stumbling up the steep brae. Each time she saw one she willed it to reach the top safely, but even though the fear of the moment when one would fall was so constantly with her, she was still unprepared for the horror of seeing Mr. Pearson's big brown Jackie-boy go down.

The crash of the big body, the threshing hooves and the ghastly tangle of great brown limbs in the traces, came with a numbing shock to her. Sickened, she watched the horse's frantic efforts to rise, its mouth opening grotesquely on a great double row of teeth as it screamed with pain; then her view was blocked by men and boys who appeared from nowhere, crowding round Jackie-boy and blurring the sharpness of his screaming with their shouts. She saw a man running up the street with a gun in his hand and the sight unfroze her trance of horror. Hands over her ears to blot out the sound of the shot she ran wildly from the pain and terror of Jackie-boy and from the murder that was about to take place.

Going down the street with her basket that day, she thought that writing her book was the only thing she had really enjoyed that winter—that, and going to

Grandma's in Edinburgh for Christmas. Grandma's had been fun with all the aunts and uncles singing the good tunes like "Gospel Bells" and "There's Honey in the Rock, My Brother," from the Redemption Song Book, and Great-Aunt Kate having hysterics when her father and Uncle George went out to the pub for a drink and screaming to everyone that they had gone to the House of the Devil.

Then her father had come back and made Great-Aunt Kate dance a jig with him, so that they all nearly died laughing at him. Even Great-Aunt Kate laughed in the end. But when he sang "Kathleen Mavourneen" specially for her because her name was really Kathleen, she cried and said,

"Patrick McShane, it's the Devil that speaks through you to make me sin by grieving for the lost beauty of my youth."

"Not at all," said he, "for the Devil was ever shamed by Truth, and isn't that the great beauty that shines in your face now?"

Then she kissed him and said he was a good fellow and by God's grace he would be Saved yet. And all the aunts smiled and whispered among themselves the shame it was that such a charming man should be a poor Sinner, and she could see that each one of them was determined she would be the one to Save him. They all liked her father at Grandma's.

The memory of what he had said to Great-Aunt Kate recalled with sudden, sharp remorse the lies she had

had to tell to keep her book a secret from him, and miserably she tried to think of something that would ease the burden of her shame, for it was beginning to weigh her down.

There were a lot of things about her that her father liked. He liked the energy she put into everything she did. He enjoyed hearing her quick tongue get the better of the Others in an argument, and sometimes when she capered about to let the excitement out of her, he laughed till he cried at the wild things she did. But there was one thing he admired that she didn't have, and that was courage. She was terribly afraid of pain and it was only when she was too excited to care about being hurt that she could do dangerous things.

She tried to hide this from him, of course, because he had no time for cowards, and he always acted as if he didn't see when she was frightened. But she was uneasily aware that he knew very well she only pretended to be brave, and it occurred to her then how pleased he would be if she did something dangerous that would make it look as if she really did have courage—surprised, too, as if he had been given an unexpected present.

And suddenly she saw that this was the idea she had been looking for. If she sprang a pleasant surprise like this on him it *would* be like giving him a present—something extra from her to him to make up for the secret she had held back.

Immediately, because it was the thing she feared

most, she thought of the big boys' slide. She could see it in front of her, running like a strip of black glass from the grocer's down to Miss McKay's sweetie-shop. There was a group of boys round it, big broad-shouldered boys from the top class at school and even some who had left school, and every few seconds one would go hurtling down it, crouched low and yelling hoarsely. No girls or small boys ever went on the slide. The big boys made sure of that by charging down it behind anyone foolish enough to try and sending them flying into the frozen gravel at the edge of the road.

She stood at the edge of the group and watched, her stomach tight with fear at the prospect of even setting foot on the glassy strip and all the brightness of her idea dimmed over with the shame of her cowardice. An elbow dug suddenly and painfully into her ribs brought her gasping round, face to face with Billy Carstairs. He pushed her, one hand flat against her face, the other jerking the shopping basket out of her grasp.

"Gerroff, you! Y'r in the way o' my run, see! G'wan!"

He followed her up, shouting, as she staggered from the push, and with a sweep of his arm tossed her basket high over her head. He was the biggest bully in the village, Billy Carstairs with his big, handsome head crowned with tight red curls. She hated him and she was terrified of his strength, but she was even more afraid of the evil something she sensed in the contrast between the noble head and the apelike features of his big face. It was pushed jeeringly into hers as she backed, the skin of it unhealthy white and spattered with freckles like the skin of a new potato that still had specks of earth clinging to it. In despair, she swung wildly out at it with both fists, missed, and felt the hard flat of his hand slap agonizingly against her left ear.

Too dazed by the impact to realize how she had got there, she found herself in the centre of a yelling, jostling crowd of boys. She was pushed, bounced and pulled backwards and forwards between them. The humiliation of it transmuted her fear into a frenzy of rage and she fought viciously against the strong clutch of the hands mauling at her. A twist that brought her clear for a second gave her a chance of escape. She seized it, charged head down through the bodies in a rush that brought her clear of them.

The slide lay right in her path but she had run a dozen feet of its length before she realized she was on it. To try and check her flight then without crashing on the slippery surface was an impossibility, and instinctively she struck out with her right foot, at the same time bracing back on her left foot so that her run was converted into a long, smooth glide. There was no time for fear. The end of the slide was looming up, the black sticky patch where she would have to do the quick foot-change again or crash face down on the road's rough surface. She timed it perfectly, even to the tapering-off of her run at the end into a steady trot.

With the release of tension, excitement welled up in her throat and burst out into a shout of triumph as she turned to face the boys at the top of the slide. They yelled back, waving and beckoning to her, and realizing that their mood had changed she ran towards them. Only Billy Carstairs was still hostile. The others were laughing at what she had done.

"Ye're a right strong wee bitch," one boy said, and another one said, "She's a wee hell-cat, ye mean. See the scratches she gied me!"

They were ready to let her have another shot at the slide—"if ye're no' feared," one of them added tauntingly.

"A' course I'm no' feared," she retorted.

Her mother would have given her a row if she had heard her talking roughly like the village boys, but talking like them was part of the excitement of the challenge she felt as she took her place in the line-up for the next run at the slide. It wasn't so easy the next time, however, without the impetus of her first run at it; nor the next time either, nor even the time after that. And lacking the flood of rage that had carried her down the first time, she had time to be afraid of the speed of her rush down the slide. But she stuck at it, cheered on by the encouraging laughter of the big boys and counting the fear as the price to be paid for her achievement.

She forgot all about the grocery basket and the messages she was supposed to take home. She was too absorbed even to connect the growing dusk and the appearance of the lamplighter to light the gas-lamp beside the slide with the fact that the shops would be

94

closing down. It was only when the boys began to drift away by ones and twos into the dusk that she realized how late it was, and in a flurry of apprehension, snatched up her basket and ran for home. Her triumph was too great and too recent, however, to be much affected by the thought of the telling-off she would get for forgetting the messages. She danced up the road, swinging the basket and singing to herself, and when she came to the front gate, ran up the path with her story bursting to be told.

They were all in the kitchen, her father and mother and William and the Others. Breathlessly, before her mother could demand to know where she had been, she blurted out,

"I'm sorry I forgot about the messages, Mam. I was sliding and it was great and I just forgot till the shop was shut. I'm sorry, Mam."

"Sliding?" her mother repeated. "You were sliding all this time? Let me see your shoes."

Her mother's voice was quiet, but she didn't have to shout. The words were reproach enough and the barb of dismay they struck through her deflated all her triumph. She had clean forgotten the orders they were under not to damage their shoes by sliding! Without a word she bent and took off her shoes and handed them to her mother. The soles were badly scarred and when she saw them her mother's face twisted as if she was going to cry.

"Bridie—oh Bridie!" she said. "Why *did* you? You

95

know we can't afford any more shoes this winter!"

There was nothing she could say. She could only stand silently there in the puddle of her shame and let the guilt grow fierily in her face. Her father hadn't said a word but now, with a grim look at her, he took the shoes in his hand and said soothingly to her mother,

"Don't upset yourself, Agnes, it's not too bad. I'll put some studs in the soles and that'll preserve what's left of them."

It took only a few minutes after that, when the last and the box of tackets had been fetched, for her father to cover the soles of her shoes with a close, neat pattern of metal. His face still grim as he handed them to her he asked,

"And where *were* you sliding, miss?"

The guilt feelings had died down with the covering-up of the damage to her shoes. She was no longer in the black books, she felt, and eagerly she answered,

"On the big boys' slide!"

Her answer startled him. "The one down the street?" he asked. "Where all those great louts skylark about?"

She nodded, smiling up at him. "I went on it hundreds of times," she boasted. "Fast, real fast, right to the very end."

"But these boys knock the little ones about if they try to go on their slide," her mother put in.

"Och, aye," she said casually. "They tried it on me—that Billy Carstairs did, anyway—but I fought him."

Her father's mouth twitched at the corners as he

96

said, "Seems to me that would all take a bit of courage."

"I wasn't scared," she told him. "Not once. I wasn't scared at all."

"Well, well," he said, and then again thoughtfully, "Well, well." Then he grinned at her and patted her on the shoulder. "Good for you, Sergeant McGra. Good for you!" and she nearly burst with pride at the look on his face.

She had done it—paid back the debt she owed him with the pleasure of the surprise she could see written there! She felt the expression on her own face giving away her feelings and knelt quickly to lace her shoes in case he guessed what she was thinking.

"You'll go like a shot from a gun if you try to slide with those studs in your shoes," his voice came from above her. "They'll fix your sliding for you."

She had no intention of sliding in the tackety shoes, of course. She would crash for certain if she did, for she would never be able to control the added speed they would give. But the feeling of triumph was still strong on her and as she stood up, stamping her feet so that the tackets clattered on the kitchen floor, she could not resist the temptation to boast,

"I like going fast. I could do fine with a slide in these."

Her father gave her a long look, lips pursed, eyebrows raised. "Off you go and slide then," he said quietly at last.

97

She gaped at him. "I'll fall," she said stupidly.

"Very likely." He was not smiling now. His eyes were boring, cold and hard, into hers. "But you're not afraid of that, surely?"

There was nothing to do then but to accept the challenge in the words. Pride wouldn't let her back down from it—not with all of them watching her and him waiting for her to show how brave she really was—but as she went slowly toward the kitchen door, all the old terror of the slide came flooding back with an impact that made her stomach heave with sickness. The excuse that it was too dark to slide now flashed into her mind and she looked back with the words ready on her lips.

"Bridie!" her mother exclaimed. "What's wrong with the child? Look at her, Patrick; she's white as paper!"

Her father looked steadily at her. "Well?" he asked and she knew he was offering her a last chance to admit herself a liar and a coward. She almost took it, but pride came to her aid, stiffening her back and stretching the muscles of her face in an attempt at a grin.

"I'm all right. I'm fine," she said. "I was just thinking how many times I'd slide, that's all."

It was a poor attempt that wouldn't have deceived her mother, let alone her father. She realized that even as she spoke, but he nodded all the same and flashed an answering grin across the room at her.

"That's the spirit," he said approvingly. "That's my Bridie girl," and she went out, letting the warm wave of his approval carry her quickly into the frosty night.

98

She did fall on the slide. Over and over again her fear and the slippery plates of metal combined to betray her and she crashed heavily on her back or on her hands and knees. But the pride that had sent her out again brought her up after each fall, and in spite of the bruises and the tears that started hot from her eyes and trickled cold down her cheeks, pride kept her going for try after try at the glassy-black length of the slide. But still, despite her fear of it and the problems of balance she had to overcome, a part of her mind persisted in wondering why her father had not been angry with her for refusing to admit she had lied.

He hated lies. He knew very well it was only pride that had sent her out again with a lie on her lips—and yet he had approved of her refusal to back down from it and admit she was afraid. Why?

Through the confusion of pain from each fall and the terror of facing up again to each new attempt at the slide, she wrestled with the problem, but it was not until she had taken her first successful run at the slide and was gliding swiftly down the whole length of it that she hit on the answer. As her stomach muscles that had been knotted tight with fear relaxed in the flying thrill of her speed, it flashed through her mind that with no fear neither would there have been any of this glory in overcoming. And in the same flash of perception, everything else became clear to her.

Her father had known that pride could stiffen her nerve enough to conquer her fear of the slide—just as it had helped her to hide her fear on all the other occasions he had pretended not to notice. So it wasn't just that he had been being kind at these times and despising her underneath for being a coward! He had been giving the pride that was in her a chance to fight her cowardice.

And that was why he hadn't been angry over her lie! He knew it wouldn't be a lie any more if she could discover for herself that that pride could be as good as courage any day. That was why he had approved when she refused to back down from it!

It never occurred to her then that she could have cheated her way out of the whole situation simply by kicking the studs in her shoes on the road to mark them as if she had been sliding. It was only long afterwards that this thought occurred to her and she was thankful for that, for if she had cheated then she would have been shamed by the look her father gave her when she came home and announced that she had gone right down the long slide on her tackety shoes and hadn't been scared.

As it was, the look of smiling pride on his face as she spoke was all she had hoped for. And later on that night, as the knowledge of how well he had understood and allowed for her fears expanded into the realization that there was no longer any need of a pretence of courage with him, she felt almost giddy with relief. When the wireless was turned on she began to dance and caper outrageously in time to the music, making such a nuisance of herself that she was sent to bed early as a punishment.

She went unrepentant, still celebrating in her mind her release from the burden of her cowardice and the new understanding with her father that had happened because of it. It was one of the best things that had ever happened to her, and certainly the greatest event of that particular winter.

8

It was in the spring that her father fell ill again; not
the pleasant spring of new grass and the clean-moss
smell of primroses, but the raw cold bluster of March
days with sleety winds that froze all warmth from the
flesh.

The men of a road-mending gang found him where
he had fallen unconscious by the roadside, and carried
him home between them. His face was grey and his
breathing was between a gasp and a groan. His hands,
purple with cold, hung slack down between the arms
of the men. He had lain for hours in the sleety wind
before they found him.

Her mother made no fuss. Quietly she ordered them
all upstairs, and from the window of the big front room
they saw one of the men running heavily down toward
the doctor's house. Nobody spoke and Bridie was glad
of the silence for the groaning, grey-faced burden the
men had carried in had frightened her beyond any
power of coherent thought.

They saw the doctor's car arrive. He got out, a sharp-faced jaunty young man so unlike shambling old Doctor McLaren that it was hard to believe he was a proper doctor. A murmuring went on downstairs and when it stopped they saw the doctor leave again. Gradually they all crept back downstairs and sat down quietly in the kitchen. Dusk was drawing down outside and the room was dim. Bridie chose the dark corner farthest away from the window and settled back into the shadows.

Her mother was moving quietly about, putting the kettle on the fire, taking down the tea caddy, measuring tea into the pot. On a chair by the big brass bed in the corner sat Mr. Muir, his wooden legs stretched stiffly out in front of him. Her father lay in the bed. His face was only a dark blur but every so often there was a white gleam of teeth from it as he turned his head on the pillow and groaned.

When he groaned Mr. Muir sat forward quickly and said, "Now, Patrick! Hold on, Patrick!" and her mother stopped dead in whatever she was doing. When the groaning died away she began the soft movements again and Mr. Muir sat back in his chair. It seemed to go on like that for a long time but it could not really have been very long for it was still not properly dark outside when the ambulance men came.

They seemed to appear out of nowhere. Suddenly the kitchen light was on and men in dark-blue uniforms were crowding in. The kitchen bustled into life: men's voices, feet scraping on the linoleum, manoeuvring of a

103

stretcher, a question shouted from the kitchen door and answered from outside; a man in dark blue bending over her, a face smiling from under a peaked cap and a voice saying, *"Cheer up, my wee hen, we'll have him fine in nae time at a'."* It was all over before she realized that her father was gone. Her mother was smoothing down the bed and the kitchen was back to normal. It was hard to believe it had all happened.

Maybe this was how it had happened when he had been ill before. She took heart from that, remembering how like his usual self he had been when he came back that time, and joined in the questioning that was going on round her mother.

Yes, her mother was saying, they had taken him to the Military Hospital. No, she didn't know how long he'd be away but they had good doctors there, perhaps it wouldn't be long. They were to be good and not worry him by quarrelling among themselves and no, they couldn't visit him, but she would go often and tell them how he was getting on. Would he be home in time to make the dolly's cradle he had promised Moira for her birthday?

They all waited for the reply to that one. Moira's birthday was at the end of May, and it would take him a little time to make the cradle. Yes, her mother thought he would be home in time for that and Bridie felt the answer like a reprieve to her secret fears because it was as good as a promise that he would get better.

She went off to bed with the Others, all four of them

chattering like starlings with the excitement of what had happened, but at the kitchen door something made her turn and look back. Her mother was standing with her face in her hands and her shoulders were shaking. It spoiled the picture she had built up for herself. It brought back the fall of the god into a man, groaning and grey with pain, and all the secret fears that had beset her. For a moment she hesitated at the door, then pity conquered her resentment and she crossed quickly to put her arms round her mother.

Her mother's body stiffened as she touched it, then the stiffness relaxed and she took her hands away from her face. It was wet with tears but there was a smile struggling weakly through them. She wiped them away with the back of her hand.

"It'll be all right, lovey," she said gently. "God wouldn't lay more on us than we could bear."

It was on the tip of Bridie's tongue to say that you couldn't trust a rotten old bully like God, but she bit it back in time. There had been enough trouble already about her and God. She ran upstairs wondering if there would be flowers on the cradle like the ones her father had carved on William's cradle when he was a baby, and whether it would be big enough to hold the baby doll they all had a share in because it had been Mammy's doll too, and Grandma's before that and even Great-Grandma Taylor's dolly as well when she had been a little girl in the olden days.

Upstairs she spoke to the Others about it, and they

got the baby doll out of its big white box that was like the coffin Mrs. Tait's dead baby had been buried in, and measured the size the cradle would have to be. Then Nell wrote the measurements down because she always had to be the boss in everything they did together.

"Nell needs a firm hand on her," her father had always said, but now that he was away there was no one to stop Nell being bossy. It was Nell who decided what games they would play after school, who was on which side and what the rules were to be, and it was always Nell who gave out the parts when they acted stories upstairs in the big front room before they went to bed. Aileen and Moira didn't argue with her because Aileen was too timid and Moira had so many private thoughts to keep her company that she didn't care who was boss anyway, but she hated being ordered about and was always arguing with Nell.

Except on Sundays, of course, when they went out hunting for violets or primroses or birds' nests, because Nell knew every bird and leaf and flower for miles around and all the best places to search for them. They were in her private kingdom then, and anything she didn't know about it, she made up. If there were no violets out at Castlebrae she would say, "There's lovely big violets out on the hawthorn bank at Craigdun," and nobody could contradict her because Craigdun was five miles away and she was the only one who had roamed that far. Or if they found a strange plant she would say right away, "I know that—it's Wandering Sailor," or maybe, "That's Maids in Mourning."

She always thought of peachy names even if she did make them up, and when she spoke of these banks of flowers that were in bloom when nothing else was out they sounded as mysterious as some dream-garden she had seen once, long ago and far away—a garden so beautiful that you knew the thought of it was always in her mind. But it was only a dream and she could never go back to it though she longed for it so much that she kept pretending she knew how to get there.

They found a lot of nests that spring, and at each find Nell made them all swear a solemn oath not to tell a soul where the nest was. It was the village boys she was afraid of, in case they discovered the nest and harried it. They would do horrible things then, like squashing the baby birds flat under their big, tackety boots or stabbing their eyes out with thorns, and so, because William was too young to understand about keeping a secret, they never let him see exactly where a nest was.

There was never any question of leaving him behind, all the same, even though he couldn't walk nearly as far as they did. They wheeled him in the old go-chair on the smooth parts of the way, and when the ground was too rough for that they took turns of carrying him piggyback. And that was one thing Nell couldn't boss her about.

She could say, "Do this about the bairn," or "Do that with the bairn," but it made no difference to William.

He was too used to her and her father to do what Nell wanted all of a sudden. The Others could talk about "the bairn" as much as they liked but now that their father wasn't in charge William only did what *she* wanted him to do. He was her bairn till their father came home, and she wished desperately there was some way of explaining to him when that would be.

Every time he asked, "When's my daddy comin' *back?*" she tried a new way of explaining weeks and months to him, but William was only four and a bit and he couldn't understand what she meant. And she couldn't say "Soon," or "Tomorrow," because that wouldn't be true. Moira's birthday had come and gone and still he wasn't home because, her mother said, there were complications and the doctors were going to do an operation to get rid of them. After that he would be all right but he would have to stay in the hospital to rest after the operation. She tried, "After my birthday," and gave William one of her pencils to score off each day in the calendar till it was the twentieth of July, and then the day came and she was nine and still he wasn't home.

"It's to be a surprise," she told William then. "You're not to ask any more because every morning after now we might get a surprise when we come downstairs and find him in the kitchen. You might even look up one day when you're playing outside and see him coming round the corner of our own street!"

The idea caught her own fancy and when she was outside playing after that she kept stealing glances towards the end of the street in case she might see him turning the corner, just as she had described it to William. And that was how it happened after all. She looked up one day and saw him coming round the corner at the end of the street. She had been skipping and she stopped dead with the rope falling in a tangle at her feet. Her heart gave a bound that was like a great painful blow driven into her chest, and she gasped with the force of it.

He saw her and waved and shouted, and then she was running along the street calling out to him in a sobbing jumble of words and he caught her as she crashed into him and held her, and the jumbled words and sobs were still pouring out of her and he was saying over them, "Hush, lovey, hush—you'll hurt yourself. Hush!" Then all of a sudden the strength seemed to go out of her legs. She was being held close to him with a button of his jacket pressing sharply against her cheek, but that was all she felt for now there was nothing in her mind but a beautiful blank and her body felt as light as a feather drifting in air.

Afterwards, when she had a chance to look at him properly, she saw that he looked different. The brown of his face had a yellowish tinge and his skin had a smooth, waxy look about it.

"You're different," she said, touching his face with

the tips of her fingers. The feel of the waxy-looking skin made her suddenly shy, as she had been one day when she was little and had lost him in a crowd, and, touching a stranger under the impression it was her father, had found an unknown face looking down at her. A flicker of the panic that had gripped her then passed over her, and breathing hard to overcome the sudden shyness, she asked, "Will you be brown again soon, like you used to be?"

"A few walks along the beach'll soon sort that," he said. He was smiling and his teeth were as white as ever. There were the same deep lines on either side of his mouth and the same crinkling of the skin round his eyes. "When d'you go back to school—next week, is it?" he asked. She nodded and he went on, "Right then, Sergeant McGra—marching orders! Home from school every day at the double, then quick march for both of us along the beach from Smuggler's Rocks to the bathing huts. Right?"

"Right!" she said.

"And then on Sunday I'll march you off your feet as far as Miller's Bay," he told her. "And if the weather holds, I'll be as brown as a nut by then."

The weather held. Every day at the beginning of that September was a shining calm of blue and gold, and they marched with the sunshine streaming over them like banners along the edge of the sea creaming up to the dark gold of the sand, singing the "Soldiers'

110

Song" and skiffing small, pink-and-brown veined pieces of rock into the waves. She told him about her book, shamefully muttering out a confession of her lies and secrecy, but all he said was,

"Everyone's entitled to a private place in the mind, lass, so you haven't wronged me with your secret. It's yourself you've wronged, for every lie you told has brought its own punishment of unhappiness to you."

And that was all the reproach he ever gave her, but farther along the beach because he could see she was still downcast, he stopped and sat down on a rock and said, "Come on, now, sit down and I'll sing to you. What song would you like?"

She asked for "She moves through the Fair" and her father sang it, his hands on his knees and his face turned to look out along the red-and-gold path the setting sun had laid across the still waters of the Firth. A quiet song, it was, a sad and lovely song with plaintive notes that trembled sweetly on the air and melted gently away into the calm of the dying day. Her father's face, turned away from her as he sang, was outlined strong and dark against the evening light, and watching it as she listened to the quiet sadness of his voice she wished that his singing to her at that time and in that place would never end. But there was no fierceness of longing in the wish for the song's gentleness had laid its spell on her, and moreover, she knew as certainly as she had ever known anything that she

111

would no more forget the song or the time and manner of its singing than she would ever forget her father himself.

The next day was a Sunday and they all went down to the beach together, except for her mother who couldn't walk far because of her rheumatism. "We'll walk to Miller's Bay," said her father, but the Others wanted to play at making sea gardens so he set off with her and William.

William rode on his shoulders part of the way, laughing at being so high and holding out his hands to the starry scatter of little white flowers on the bramble bushes at the top of the sand dunes. They stopped at the bay and leaned against the seawall while William played at making sand pies with an old pail he had found.

A beach photographer came along and took a snap of him, then he turned and pointed his camera at her and her father. Her father didn't like being photographed and when the man pointed his camera at them she stood up straight beside him, looking sternly at the man and ready to move away as soon as her father gave the word. But the shutter clicked before he had time to say anything, and her father only shrugged and took the little ticket the man gave him. Then they went back along the beach to find the Others, and just before it was time to go home the photographer came up to her father and handed him the prints of the two photographs.

He took them, smiling at the one of William and passed it for them to see. They all clustered round, peering and smiling at the picture of the skinny little boy crouched so solemn and earnest over his crooked little castle of sand, then her father handed her the other snapshot. She looked at it, then looked at it again with astonishment gripping her suddenly like a hand at her throat as she realized, for the first time, how closely she resembled her father. And it was not only in the features that the likeness lay, for the expression on her father's face was hers too. Her eyes gazed levelly from the photograph with the same air of challenge, her mouth was set with the same firm determination as his.

Slowly she raised her eyes from the photograph and met his looking down at her. It flickered over her mind that they were the same grey-green as her own, and as she smiled involuntarily in response to the amusement in his face she wondered if there was the same light of laughter in her eyes as there was in his.

There was nothing in the world so fascinating as the light that danced in his eyes when he laughed, and the thought that she might look like this also made her blush with sudden confused pleasure. A little breathlessly, because the feeling made her shy, she asked,

"Am I like you like that—I mean smiling, as well?"

"Indeed you are—you're liker me than I am myself!" he said, and grinned broader than ever at her as he handed over the money for the photographs. The

113

photographer smiled too, glancing from her to her father, and said, jokingly, "Aye, ye couldna deny that yin, mister!"

She felt the blush deepening on her face and her father said, only half-joking now, "Hey, hey—what's this? You're not ashamed to be like your dad, are you?"

He put his finger under her chin to tilt her face up to his, but for the moment she had stood all she could of this peculiar mixture of pleasure and embarrassment and she broke away from him, running up the beach with her hand pushed down hard over the photograph in the pocket of her dress, and chanting loudly as she ran,

"I'm goin' to be first home! I'm goin' to be first home!"

The Others took up the cry, racing after her and jostling to outpace her up the path, and in the running fight of laughter and pushing and shouting that carried them homeward, she buried the confusion of feelings that had gripped her so strangely. Later on, she promised herself, when she could be alone in some quiet place, she would take them out again along with the photograph. Then she would be able to think properly over this discovery of her likeness to her father.

She showed her mother the photograph when she got home. "I'll keep it for you till I can get it put in a little frame, then you can have it back," her mother told her. But she never did get it back. She was afraid to ask for it for the next day her father went back to the hospital in the doctor's car. It was just for a little check-up, her mother said, but a week from that day they came down-stairs and found the kitchen empty, and they went out into the back garden to play till their mother came back from wherever she was.

When they heard the car drawing up at the front door Nell shouted to them all to come right away and see who it was, but she wasn't going to let Nell order her about and so she hung back while the Others rushed William round to the front of the house. She gave them just long enough to satisfy pride, then she ran to the front of the house herself in time to see the smooth black back of the car disappearing along the street. She ran into the house and saw her mother and Mrs. Wallace standing in front of the kitchen fireplace and as she stood staring at them, Mrs. Wallace said,

"Puir bairns. Puir bairns."

Her mother said, *"I'll have to tell them,"* and then she told them,

"Your father's dead."

Part 2

1

When the first outburst of grief for her father was over that day she was told of his death, Bridie came back to a world that had changed in some subtle way.

Everything seemed slower and quieter than it had been before and nothing that happened seemed to connect directly with her. She saw people moving, as it were, through some transparent film that separated her from them and their voices came to her muffled as if she had gone partially deaf. There was often an unaccountable gap in time between her thought of an action and the business of performing it, so that she was sometimes puzzled to find herself in a particular place or doing a particular thing.

She began to have nightmares. At first it was only the constant iteration of a voice saying, *"Your father's dead. Your father's dead,"* that woke her, weeping. Then she found the medical book and a different nightmare began to haunt her sleep.

The book was a big, red-bound volume which she

119

knew did not belong on any of their bookshelves. It appeared in the house a week after her father's death and her mother spent a lot of time studying it. Sometimes Mrs. Soutar came in while she had the book open and then they had an argument over it. Mrs. Soutar kept saying, "Why d'you torment yourself like this, Agnes? The doctors told you there was no explaining these sudden relapses." And her mother always answered, "There must be an explanation, Lena, and I've got to find it. I can't rest till I do."

Then one day Mrs. Soutar lost patience with her and snapped, "You can pore over that blessed book till you're blue in the face but *that* won't bring Patrick back!"

Her mother, who never swore, got up and said quietly, "Get out of my house, you bitch."

Mrs. Soutar gaped at her; then she burst into tears and ran out of the house. After that she never came back and Bridie began to watch to find out where her mother kept the book hidden when she wasn't reading it.

She found it, one day when her mother was out, on a shelf of the corner cupboard in the kitchen. She was too afraid of being caught reading it to lift it down from the shelf and so she brought a chair to stand on to read it where it lay. Then she opened it and began to search, as her mother was doing, to see if she could find out why her father had died.

The diagrams in the book caught her eyes instantly.

There was one of a whole body and other, smaller ones of different limbs and sections of the body, all traced in red. She studied them, both repelled and fascinated by their shape and by the colour which she took to represent the blood she assumed must connect them all. They, at least, made some sense, but the wording of the text defeated her completely.

Nevertheless she found that she could not leave the book alone, for it seemed to her that her mother was on the right track. She had to find out why her father had died, otherwise it just didn't make sense that such a thing could happen. It was like some horrible trick that had been played on them, and so, every time she had an opportunity to do so, she continued with her secret study of the medical book.

The chair she used to stand on was only high enough to allow her to read if she stood on tiptoe, so that after a few minutes reading her legs began to tremble with the strain. The constant fear of discovery made the trembling worse once it had started, and the two things combined made her feel sick, so sick sometimes that she had to give up reading even before her mother's footsteps outside warned her it was time to jump down and pretend to be doing something else.

The nightmare that followed on from the reading always took the same form. All the men in their street—the blind men, the legless, the armless ones—were standing in a silent, motionless group outside the wooden fence surrounding the little graveyard in front of the church. They were all looking in the same direction. Even the blind men among them had their heads turned towards the bare plot of grass in the centre of the graveyard. The something they were gazing at was a dismembered body. She could see all the different parts of it, each lying in the pool of its own blood, and as she watched she saw that each of the dismembered limbs was moving as if it was still alive. Then she became aware that the sound she could hear was the head crying feebly aloud, and with a rush of pity she realized that the body *was* alive and that its separated head was crying desperately for help.

None of the cripples moved to help it. She cried urgently to them, *"It's still alive! Help it, please help it!"* But the group of misshapen men, as if they had not heard her, continued to stand there as silent and motionless as some grotesque waxworks show.

She had to help it. It was impossible to leave the poor thing there, crying out like that. She crept towards it. The head turned and looked at her. She saw her own face and realized that the thing was herself, and from this last unbearable horror she pried herself, screaming, into wakefulness again.

The memory of the nightmare was always with her in her secret searches of the medical book; and, although the horror of it was less in the daylight, it was still enough to add to the feeling of physical sickness that always overcame her in the end. It was enough, too, to make her want to confide in her mother, and beg her to

122

put away the book that was troubling them both so much. Yet she never did this, for her mother had changed from the kind and cheerful Mammy she had always been able to turn to in trouble before.

Nor was this simply because her mother was always quiet and pale now, and dressed in black. It was much more because the gentleness that had always been the wonderful thing about her could no longer be relied on.

There were times now when she would be going quietly about her work as usual and suddenly she would stop as if she had been struck, and put her hand to her side, leaning backwards as if her back hurt. A cry as weak and helpless as the mew of a kitten would come from her pale lips; then her face would crack and crumple across into a grotesque, weeping mask and all her gentleness would vanish in the raw fury of the outburst of grief that followed.

The intensity of her mother's emotions frightened Bridie. It frightened them all so that, although they wept in sympathy with her at the beginning of each outburst, it always finished up for them in tears of terror. In the grip of this terror they would try to pull her hands away from her face as they begged her wildly not to cry, and in the end she would hear them and try to bring herself under control again. But there was one terrible occasion when they were all babbling and pulling at her like this and she shrieked out suddenly,

"There's no God! THERE'S NO GOD!"

William stared up at her in bewilderment. The Others shrank back from her with horrified disbelief in their faces. Bridie could feel the same expression showing on her own face and the feeling persisted even after her mother had collapsed into tears again and wept herself out.

It had been difficult enough already to reconcile her mother's normal, gentle self with the wild fury of her grief and it was even more difficult after this demented shriek had come from her. As Bridie puzzled over it, it began to seem to her that these furious onslaughts of grief must be the result of some force outside her mother—some monstrous thing that had crept in from outside and was lying constantly in ambush waiting its chance to attack her.

She began to be afraid for her mother, afraid that the monster might kill her. People did die of grief. She had read about it often enough, and now the times she had the nightmare of the body in the churchyard began to be interspersed with those of another nightmare in which she dreamed about the thing that was trying to kill her mother.

She was in the kitchen with her mother. It was very quiet and the beast was waiting outside but her mother didn't know it was there. She had her back to the door, and as Bridie watched, the door began to inch open. Something appeared round it, close to the floor. It was a face, neither animal nor human—a dark face, human in shape and skin but grinning thin, sharp, animal fangs at her. It knew she was there and it knew also that she could neither move nor speak. Its eyes glittered at her, signalling a horrible glee at the thing it was about to do. She struggled madly to release the lock on her speech and as the beast sprang she managed a shriek of warning to her mother.

It came too late. Her mother swung round only to receive the impact of the beast against her chest. It clung to her, burying its long sharp fangs in her flesh. She cried thinly, the weak mewing cry that the beast's fangs always wrung from her to begin with. Her hand flew to her side and her face cracked and crumpled across with the shock of the attack. And then, as the tearing and worrying at her flesh began, she sobbed and shrieked with the pain of the beast's fangs devouring her.

The nightmare did not finish there for she was aware that when the beast had finished with her mother it would attack her. She struggled to move so that she could escape it and sometimes she succeeded before her turn was imminent, but sometimes it was not until the beast was scrabbling bloodily across the floor towards her that she managed to escape into wakefulness. And sometimes as she lay trembling and awake in the darkness, it seemed to her that the beast had pursued her even out of sleep for she could hear the sound of sobbing still.

It always took her several moments to realize that the sobbing was coming from the little back room where her mother had slept since the big brass bed in the kitchen

125

had been taken down after her father died; and when her mind had cleared enough to grasp this she would lie uneasily wondering whether she should go through and try to comfort her. With the thought of the beast still vivid in her mind she was too frightened to get out of bed, but one night the sobbing was so desolate that she could not bear to lie and listen to it any longer.

She slipped out of bed and padded softly through to the back bedroom. In the little light that filtered into it she could see her mother's head on the pillow, but not her face, for the bedclothes were drawn up close round it. She knelt down beside the bed and put a hand timidly out to her mother's face. It was hot, burning hot to the touch, and wet with tears.

"Mammy," she whispered, "please don't cry, Mammy."

Her mother became very still. Seconds ticked by and then, with despairing quietness she said,

"Go back to bed. You don't understand."

She did, she *did* understand! She knew about the beast that was tearing at her mother, she knew what the pain was like! She wanted to tell her about it. She wanted to tell her she knew it was there. She wanted her to know that she would kill it if she could, but there was no way of explaining all that. She could only say desperately,

"I *do*, oh Mammy, I *do* understand!"

Her mother forced herself up on to one elbow. Her other hand shot out and clamped round the wrist of the hand Bridie had stretched out to her face. She pulled her close.

"Do you? Do you *really* understand?"

The heat of her mother's body came out of the bed-clothes in a wave—the same unnaturally fiery heat that was in the hand clutching her wrist. She was held close in its grip, terrified by the force of the gesture and the sudden knowledge of the fever that was burning in her mother, and appalled beyond thought by the despera-tion in her voice. She could say nothing. Fear and pity between them had paralyzed her power of speech, and after a moment her mother released her hand. In a flat, tired voice she said,

"It's all right, dearie. Go back to bed now."

Bridie went back to bed and lay listening to the silence that came from the back bedroom. Her wrist was still tingling from the grasp her mother had laid on it. She nursed it under the covers with her other hand and, still appalled at the loneliness that could make a grown-up person like her mother snatch so desperately at understanding from even a child of her age, she vowed silently,

"I'll never marry. I'll never marry because my husband might die, and then I couldn't bear to be as unhappy as Mam."

The realization of how her mother was suffering over-whelmed her to such an extent that the sharp ache of desolation she had carried inside her since her father died was temporarily stilled. But when she fell asleep again that night, she had the nightmare from which she used to wake weeping when she heard the voice saying over and over again, "Your father's dead." This time, however, she only dreamt that she had wakened.

Her father was standing at the bedroom door when she woke up crying from the dream. He was holding up a lighted candle to see if any of them were still awake the way he used to do when there had been trouble in the street or a thunderstorm or anything else that might have frightened them. She jerked out of bed and ran to him and put her arms round him, and he was warm and real and living under her hands.

"Hey, hey!" he said. "What's this then? And what are *you* crying for, a big girl like you?"

"They said you were dead," she told him, feeling herself blush because it sounded so silly, and he laughed and said,

"Away and don't be daft, girl! And get back into bed before you catch a cold."

She went back to bed and fell asleep again, and when she woke up in the morning still feeling warm inside and out with happiness and relief, she remembered the dream. And then she remembered that he *was* dead. And that was worse, far worse, than any of the nightmares had ever been.

2

William had still not grasped what the word "dead" meant and she found it very difficult to explain to him, but she managed it at last when one of Nell's rabbits died.

Nell had a whole menagerie of pets in the hut at the foot of the garden, most of them creatures she had found lying injured or caught in traps. None of them had much chance of recovering from their injuries, so that she was forever fussing over some corpse or other. The rabbit that died had appeared perfectly healthy, however, only the day before, and she had it cradled in her arms and was weeping bitterly over it when they found her. William stared solemnly from her to the rabbit and then said to Bridie,

"Make it better."

"Nobody can make it better," she told him. And because it had always been her father who had helped Nell to doctor her pets, had to catch herself up from adding, "—not even Dad."

"It's dead," she explained. "Touch it and see."

"Don't want to." William's voice quavered with fright and he backed a step away but she caught his right hand and pulled him back. She laid his hand on the dead rabbit and held it there.

"It's stiff and cold, see? It won't move, never again. It's finished. We'll have to bury it in the ground and cover it up. That's what dead is."

William began to howl and struggle to get away from her but she held his hand firmly against the rabbit's corpse and repeated,

"Dead is cold and stiff and finished. Covered up in the ground. Like Dad. The rabbit's dead now, the same as Dad."

William kept howling and she had to shake him to make him listen to her. Usually she hated to see William cry but now he too was on the other side of the barrier that cut her off from everybody else, so that she couldn't feel sorry for him. Making him understand was just a thing that had to be done and all that she felt was just a vague sense of relief when he seemed to grasp at last what she was telling him.

Aileen and Moira were angry with her for making William cry, and when Moira said, "You'll get in trouble with Mam for that, Bridie McShane," they began to quarrel. Nell interrupted them.

"We'll have to have a funeral for Bluey. Stop fighting, you ones, we're going to have a funeral."

"*No!*"

They all stared at her when she shouted *"No!"* like that. Nell always had a funeral when one of her pets died. She enjoyed it, preaching and singing and praying over the grave. They had cats and rabbits and birds buried all over the garden from Nell's funerals— but this was different! She stared back at them, unable to explain how Nell's words had made her own explanation to William boomerang back on herself so that now, although they hadn't been allowed to go to their father's funeral, she was suddenly aware of the coldness and stiffness of his body in the coffin waiting to be lowered into the hole in the ground—as aware of it as if she had seen and touched it for herself.

Moira broke their uneasy silence with a shout of, "Stick, then! I'll go and get a shoe box for Bluey."

She ran off to the house. Nell and Aileen began to dig a hole under one of the currant bushes, and when Moira came back with the shoe box they buried Bluey in it. Nell prayed over the grave. She ordered them all to shut their eyes when she prayed, but Bridie kept hers open. She saw that Moira and Aileen and William looked very solemn and that Nell had an earnest, up-lifted expression on her face. But close as they all were to her, she had the curious impression that they were tiny and faraway as if she was seeing them through the wrong end of a telescope.

She blinked rapidly in sudden fear that the distorted vision meant that she was going blind, and impelled by the same fear, turned and stumbled away from the grave-side. The Others called after her, and with her fear veering into a dread that they would make her come back, she broke into a run. There was still something wrong with her sight. The bushes in the garden sprang out at her alarmingly huge, and when she swerved from them they dwindled to knee-high shrubs. When she gained the street outside and ran along it, it seemed to widen and contract in front of her while the houses on either side leaned in odd, threatening angles over her, so that her only desire became to continue running, running as fast as she could towards the safeness of open country.

When exhaustion brought her to a halt finally she was in the lane leading to Castlebrae farm, and leaning against one of the drystone dikes that bounded it on either side she was immediately and violently sick. The wall and the field towards which she bent spun round her. She closed her eyes tightly against the heaving sight of them, but in spite of her dizziness her thoughts stood out with a cold and terrible clarity.

She tried to blank them out, manoeuvring desperately in her mind to recapture the conception she had been taught of death as the little, unimportant step between life on earth and glory in Heaven, but Heaven was impossibly remote in her imagination now. It was only death she could think of for only death was real now that she really understood what it was—eyes blind, ears stopped up, senses all swallowed up in coldness and blackness, everything ending in cold, black nothing.

That was what had happened to her father—and if it could happen to him, *it could happen to her!*

In panic revulsion from the thought she jerked upright as if she could pull herself physically away from it, but even the relief of this gesture was denied her for she was pinned to the wall by a stem of brier-rose trailing across the back of her right hand. The thorns tore across her skin as she moved and with an involuntary gasp of pain she stopped to lift the stem away. The blood oozing thinly along the lines of scratches the thorns had made sprang up in separate droplets as she freed her hand. She lifted the hem of her dress to wipe the blood away but with the movement only half-completed her gaze was caught and held by the deep, dark red of the drops of blood against her skin, and like a revelation it struck her that this was the way the blood ran, drop by drop, in her veins. This was the stuff that kept her alive. This *was* her life, these shiny red drops welling from her skin, and with the inescapable fact that she would die some day still beating in her brain she was suddenly seeing them with an acuteness of vision that made it seem as if a skin had been peeled from her eyes.

Each drop, she noted, was a perfect sphere glistening with highlights and trembling minutely from the slight motion of her hand. She moved her hand a little more and the glistening globules broke into trails of brilliant red across her skin. Fascinated, she continued staring at the mysterious pattern they made till it dulled and congealed on her hand, and when she looked up from it, it was to see everything within the range of her vision with the same heightened degree of perception as she had noted the shape and colour of the drops of blood.

Some late roses still clung to the brier-stems trailing across the wall, and staring at them as if she had never seen a rose before and never would again, she noted all the minute gradations of colour in each shallow pink cup of translucent petals and the fragile network of silvery veins spreading upwards through them from the circle of miniscule yellow suns that formed its corolla.

A fly alighting on her bare knee made her glance down, and in the infinitesimal flick of time it rested there the iridescent transparence of its wings registered their whole peacock kaleidoscope of colour on her sight. Her downward glance took in the grass at her feet as now no longer a uniform mass of green but a complex intertwining of myriad-shaped stems and endlessly variegated shades of half a dozen different colours. The smell from a damp-darkened mound of earth among the grass reached her and registered in her mind with a knowledge of fertility and growth that was primeval in its intensity, for all her senses, it seemed, were sharing in this extension of their function; and when a skylark began trilling above her the sound impinged so acutely on her hearing that it seemed miraculous for such a concentration of song to be beating its way out of one tiny bird's throat.

With an effort that felt as if she herself was rooted in the soil and was tearing herself free from it, she stepped off the grass verge and moved off slowly down the lane —slowly, because her sight was so alert to everything that passed before it; slowly, because her sense of touch seemed to have become refined to the point where she felt she could distinguish even through the soles of her sandals the shape of the smallest stones under her feet; slowly, because through all her senses she was filtering into their component parts the whole vast complex of smells and sounds, shapes, colours and textures through which she moved.

All the time that she walked she could hear a refrain beating in her mind, "*I am alive! I am alive!*" And knew, without having to reason out why it should be so, that the refrain was as much an anguished protest against the fact that she would have to die some day as it was an assertion of the present miracle of being alive. Even more clearly she was aware that there was no going back now to the moment before she understood what death was and that it would happen to her. Nor did she wish to go back, for, in spite of the painful fear of death that had projected it, the miraculous sharpening of her perceptions had swung her up to a peak of exaltation beyond anything she had ever reached before.

Besides, she argued to herself, she was young. She would not die for a long time yet. But the argument did not dismiss, as she had thought it would, the vision of her own body lying as cold and stiff and blind to the world as her father's had become when he died. The fear of death at the end of the road was added to, instead, by the fear of the passage of Time along the way. Every moment that passed now, she thought in panic, would be a moment of the precious time she had left in which to be aware of everything—a moment of her life slipping away, like silk, out of her grasp.

Time, like a visible spectre, loomed up over her then and fought on equal terms with her exaltation so that she felt her brain would burst with the pressure of the battle going on inside it. And now she did want to go back—further back even than the moment before she had become aware that she too could die. But because she knew that there was no going back now, all that she could think of was that she wanted her mother, wanted her with such immediacy and desperation that she was running towards home before she was even aware of having turned in her tracks.

She reached home blown and utterly exhausted, but her sense of relief at being there was dashed from her as soon as she came into the kitchen. Her mother was seated in the armchair by the fire in the grip of one of her terrible outbursts of grief. The Others and William were clustered round her as usual, weeping with her, and in the bitterness of the moment of disappointment at finding her last refuge had failed her, Bridie broke down and wept also.

From force of habit she joined the group round her mother, but because this time her tears were for a separate cause, she found she was unaffected by her mother's grief. She was too exhausted to weep for long, but when the last tear and shudder had been squeezed out of her she continued to kneel beside her mother and to watch her, and resentment began to fill her mind as she observed the contortions of her face and the tears that spurted endlessly from the swollen sockets of her eyes. It would be no use trying to tell her mother what had happened. Her mind was closed now to everything but her own grief. She wouldn't understand because she wouldn't even listen.

Coldly and dispassionately she waited for the outburst to taper off to its end. She still felt sorry for her mother but in a detached sort of way which made her dimly aware that having once viewed her like this she could never again be so painfully involved in her emotions. It crossed her mind also as she watched that her father would have disapproved of these outbursts. He had always disliked fuss and tears.

As if the look directed on her had made her mother aware that she was being watched, she looked up suddenly. Their eyes met, and as she took in the expression on Bridie's face the quivering of her own swollen face grew still. All the blood drained from it leaving it as grey as ashes and she whispered,

"Don't look at me like that! You're just like your father!"

She rose shakily to her feet. Bridie sank back on her heels looking up at her wondering fearfully what would

come next, but her mother said nothing more. She went
out of the kitchen leaving behind her a silence into
which Nell said accusingly,

"*Now* you've done it!"

They stared at her, even William, with solemn ac-
cusation in their eyes for the way in which she had
somehow managed to upset their mother, and because
she was still confused about it herself she took refuge in
rudeness.

"Ach, mind your own business!" she snapped at Nell,
and rushed away from them out to the garden and into
the little private alley between the privet hedge and
the gooseberry bushes. Lying face down on the grass
there she thought of what her mother had said and
wished that she had had the courage to ask her for the
photograph that proved the likeness between herself
and her father, for now that it had upset her mother so
much she might tear up the photograph. A pang went
through her at the possibility and fiercely she thought,

"It wouldn't do her any good. I'm bound to go on
looking like him, and I'll think like him too if I want.
She can't stop me."

For a brilliant moment then she saw herself transformed into a veritable image of her father, speaking
like him with a commanding roar or an amused chuckle
in her voice, taking charge of situations when everybody else panicked, facing fearlessly up to the gentry or
stopping to talk kindly to crabbed old Mr. Murphy because he couldn't leave his wheelchair. Then the image

faded as the spectre of pursuing Time that had driven her home obtruded on it.

She rolled over on her back and stared despairingly up through the leaves of the gooseberry bushes at the fragmented blue of the sky. If only she could tell her father about it, ask him what to do! The words yelled in her mind but no sound came from her. He was dead, dead, dead, she told herself, deliberately ramming the words home so that she would not be tempted to try and escape into a daydream that avoided the fact.

For a long time she lay there, staring mute and miserable up into the sky. She had never missed her father so much or felt so utterly lonely without him, but whenever the rising tears threatened to overwhelm and ease her desolation she kept them stubbornly at bay. She was not going to be like her mother and spend time in weeping now that she knew how precious it was. She would hold on to the very end, even of this, and then she would be able to look back and say triumphantly that she hadn't wasted a moment of Time.

She held on grimly, and slowly the pain receded. Then she rose to her feet, shook the grass and leaves off her dress, and went briskly towards the house. The fullness of the day's sunshine fell on her as she came out of the little alley. She lifted her face towards it and the spasm of delight that shook her at its touch on her skin lifted her businesslike mood into one of lightheartedness.

She began to run and skip over the crazy-paving of

the path, and all the time as she bobbed up and down the tune of a song that her father used to sing was running through her head. She had never known the words of it properly but there was something in them about "—life was not made for sorrow," and as she remembered this she had the odd but reassuring feeling that her father knew and approved of the way she had held back her tears. And with a sudden sense of achievement it occurred to her that it was the kind of thing he might have done himself if he had been in her position.

3

That winter, the first one after her father died, she was in a lot of trouble in different ways. At home she irritated everyone with what her mother called her dreaminess, and at school she was always being blamed for laziness and inattention. There was nothing she could do about it either for it took time to get used to the clear, sharp way in which she saw things now. She simply had to stand and stare till she had absorbed the whole intricate wonder of anything that caught her eye —even the most ordinary things, she found, had a shape, a colour, a texture she had never realized before. Faces, too, were different, for somehow the barrier between other people and herself had vanished along with the skin that had been peeled from her eyes in the lane after Bluey's funeral, and now that she was back in close and direct contact with people she saw them with the same clarity of vision that applied to everything else.

It was unexpectedly horrifying in some ways, how-

141

ever, to be able to see the grown-ups around her so clearly. Suddenly, now that she was so acutely aware of the functioning of her own senses, there was a frightening significance for her in the crippled condition of the men in the street.

The group of blind men waiting patiently for the bus that would take them to work in the Poppy Factory in Edinburgh drew her eyes irresistibly every morning when she passed them on her way to school. Her run would slow to a walk, her walk come to a dead stop as she stared at the dark glasses barred black across their expressionless faces, and with a fearful growing curiosity she would wonder what lay behind them. Were the blind men's eyes still there, blank as the eyes of dead fish, or were there only blood-encrusted holes behind the dark lenses? Furtively now, when she passed one of the legless men, she would place both hands flat against her thighs so that she could feel the smooth coordination of her own muscles as she walked, and with shuddering interest would speculate on how it must feel to walk with one leg that had been abruptly severed and joined to a wooden stump. And each time she had to pass old Murphy's gate she did so now at a run.

She had never liked waiting beside her father when he stopped to talk to old Murphy, because of the rug he wore wrapped chest-high round him in his wheelchair. It had kept slipping as the old man talked and every-time it slipped down a certain length Mrs. Murphy quickly hitched it up again. She always stood by his chair, a little old Dresden doll of a woman in a long black dress with snowy-white hair piled high on her head, and she nodded all the time her father and old Murphy talked, nod-nod-nodding her snowy-white old doll's head in time to the slip-slip-slipping of the rug till it was time for the quick stoop and the hitch again.

She had wondered then if Mrs. Murphy's nodding meant that she knew what lay under the rug, and she had been afraid that the old woman kept hitching it up because it was there to hide the terrible secret of what had happened to old Murphy in the War. Now she was sure of it. There was a hole, a great big hole right through the middle of old Murphy, and that was why she ran past the house turning her head aside in case the rug slipped and she saw the hole, the terrible bloody hole right through the middle of old Murphy.

There was always something that made her stop, however, when she reached the end of the street where Mr. Lockhart had the tiny shop with the notice, *Stump-Painted Pottery*, in the window; some strange fascination that held her with her nose pressed against the glass watching Mr. Lockhart painting the pottery he sold there.

Mr. Lockhart had no left arm at all and his right arm was only a stump ending above where the elbow had been, in a tight puckering of skin like the gathered end of an oatmeal pudding. He hardly ever spoke to anyone and he never smiled, just sat there all day manipulating the paintbrush that was held in place by a strap round

143

the stump of his right arm. It was this stump itself and not the skill with which it directed the delicate tip of the brush that held her fascinated attention, and all the time that she watched it she could feel her own right hand clenching and unclenching again in instinctive protest against the monstrous fact of its missing fingers.

So absorbed was she in the movements of the stump that she failed to grasp the fact that the wrath in Mr. Lockhart's face every time she appeared at the window, was for herself; until the day that he turned and jabbed viciously with the paintbrush at the glass in front of her eyes. It all happened so swiftly, the jab of the paintbrush and the spatter of paint momentarily blinding her was so unexpected, that she reared back with terror striking like a thin, sharp knife-blade into her heart. She turned and ran, and never passed the Stump-Painted-Pottery window again without a fear of the thin blade of terror instead of a hand at the end of the puckered white stump of Mr. Lockhart's arm.

The whole street was becoming a place of terror to her, in fact, for the more she was driven by the impulse to try and experience the crippled men's deformities with her own senses, the nearer the street became to a waking version of the nightmare that ended with the discovery of herself as the dismembered body in the churchyard.

She began to avoid going out to join the Others in the games they played after school, but she still had to go out with William on Saturday mornings for he was still too young to remember all the time what she had explained to him. When he lost his temper in a game he would still scream at the children playing with him, *"I'll tell my daddy on you!"* and then they would laugh at him and jeer, *"Ye havena got a daddy. Y'r daddy's deid!"* dancing round him and chanting it over and over again till she could break through them to rescue him.

The Others joined with her on these occasions, and they fought beside her on William's behalf with a fury that took no account of the results when they were outnumbered in the battle. At home, they joined with her in a conspiracy of silence that hid from their mother the reason for all the scratches and bruises they had suffered. And yet, in spite of her despairing rage at the easy target William made, it was this very babyishness of his eventually which led to the thing that enabled her to come to some sort of terms with her horror of the crippled men.

It was getting near Christmas when it happened and almost time for the party her father had always organized in the Church Hall for the War Veterans' children. Mr. Gladsmuir, the minister, was to take charge of it instead of him that year, but their mother said they could not go because it was too soon after the funeral. William had never been to the party before. This would have been his first time at any party, in fact, and he had been looking forward to it since September when their father had first promised him he could go. He cried with such bitter disappointment when their mother said that none of them were to be allowed to attend, that she yielded to his tears at last.

"Very well," she conceded, "you can go—but only if you wear your mourning clothes."

That seemed a reasonable enough ruling to them for it was just under three months, after all, since their father had died, and it was not till after they had arrived at the hall and were mingling with all the other children that Bridie realized how conspicuous the four of them were in their black skirts and jerseys.

William, in his grey flannel suit with a black armband round the right jacket sleeve, wasn't much different from all the other little boys. She and the Others, however, were like four ungainly black crows hopping among the pale blues and greens and pinks of the other girls' party dresses, and all the time the games went on she was miserably aware of how odd they must look to the mothers sitting around watching. It didn't need their sidelong glances to tell her that the McShane children didn't belong at this party. She knew already that she didn't belong, and as game followed game the sense of not belonging to the party took more and more of a hold on her until, at last, it seemed to her that she was only on the outside looking in at it all.

She saw herself from the outside too, dancing through the moves of "The Farmer's in His Den" and "Dusty Bluebells" and heard her voice singing the words of the games, but the words and the gestures didn't belong to her. It was only a black puppet that was singing and dancing among the other children. She watched the puppet going through the motions of enjoyment and felt sad for it, jumping about and singing in a place where no one wanted it.

When the mothers began to hand round the lemonade and buns and ice cream, the Others came to sit beside her on one of the benches that ran around the walls of the room. William was away in a corner enjoying himself with a group of little boys and no one else came to sit with them. The space on the bench at either side of them cut them off from the rest of the party more obviously than the looks of the women had done. The Others could feel it now. She could see that from the red flush of embarrassment on the faces of Nell and Moira and the way Aileen's face had gone blank so that nothing could be read from it. The feeling of being on the outside looking in at everything was stronger than ever. The sadness she felt was profound now, a dull, heavy feeling that lay like a darkness on her mind.

When the last ice cream had been eaten Mr. Gladsmuir began to call on each child to do its party-piece. It was the accepted custom. Every child was supposed to do a turn at the Christmas party, but it was only as the choice moved nearer to herself and the Others that she realized what tension there was among the grown-ups in the hall. She saw the looks that passed back and forward from them to the women, the heads bent to whisper to one another. She heard the joviality of Mr.

147

Gladsmuir's voice grow false and strained as the choice came even nearer to them and realized that the adults were wondering which would be the greater blunder —to ask children in mourning to perform at a party or to make them even more conspicuous by passing over them completely.

Nell solved the problem for Mr. Gladsmuir by getting to her feet before she could be either asked or ignored. Nell never missed a chance to act, of course. She gave them "Curfew Shall Not Ring Tonight," with all the gestures and tones her mother used when she recited it to them at bedtime, and sat down to ringing applause. Aileen and Moira followed quite naturally then, Aileen with a song she had learned at school and Moira with another song and a dance to it that she had made up herself. Aileen was applauded politely but everyone clapped in time to Moira's dancing and cheered her when it was finished. Then it was her turn and she rose to her feet determined to outshine Nell with a recitation of another of her mother's poems, "The Boats of Brixham."

As she walked to the position Moira had just left she was arranging the words in her head, and she looked up the hall at the semicircle of women and children with the first two lines ready to tumble off her tongue. They were waiting, with listening faces, for her to begin, but in the split second it took for her to open her lips the lines of the poem vanished from her mind. It was her father's song that came in their place, the sad and gentle song he had sung to her that evening by the Firth when she had confessed the secret of her book to him. Without warning it came into her mind, as if the sadness that was in her had found its own voice in it, and without any volition on her own part she began to sing.

The sadness poured out of her in the song, a sadness that was somehow not only for herself now, but for them all. She saw the hall as she sang and it was no longer a big place to her, a gay and exciting party place. It was small suddenly and shabby, the floor greasy with spillings and squalid with littered ice-cream cups. But it was only with the background of her vision that she saw it for she was watching the women's faces as she sang and seeing on each one of them the shadow of the cripple that stood behind it. And she was aware too, as she sang, of the darkness outside the hall, aware of it not as the ordinary dark of night but as a great and terrible *something* surrounding them all; and her mind cried out through the song to the women that here inside the hall they were safe together in a little oasis of light in the big darkness.

They were all inside it, linked together and pushing back against the great dark outside, and a wave of compassion was carrying her forward into them, into the chain of women linked together to hold off the great world of darkness pressing in all round them. All the familiar identities she knew for them were gone, swallowed up in an overwhelming awareness of their common weakness, their common plight. And from this

149

awareness and from her compassion there was flowering such a vast, incommunicable love for them all that the song was finally choked in tears and faltered to a stop.

There was a moment of dead silence as she stood blinking and slowly assembling the realization that she was Bridie McShane making a show of herself by standing in the middle of the floor audibly crying at the Children's Party. No one moved or spoke. She got back to her seat somehow and Mr. Gladsmuir called heartily to the next child to come and do his piece. He did a recitation popular on such occasions and there was laughter at all the right places in it. But behind the laughter there were more of the sidelong glances at her and there was a shifting and whispering among the women that continued till there were no more performers left and the party was over.

None of the Others spoke to her on the way home, but neither did they jeer at her afterwards for the show she had made of herself and she was intensely relieved at this. It was difficult enough to explain what had happened to herself, never mind being forced to do so to the Others over a barrage of jeers; for now that the moment's insight the song had given to her sadness was gone, she had no conception of why she had felt that rush of compassion for the women in the hall or of why she had reached out from it to identify herself with them.

Even though she could not explain them, however, she retained a clear remembrance of the feelings she had experienced then, and all the rest of that winter after her father died she relived them briefly each evening when the light was put on in the kitchen and the blinds drawn against the dark outside. At the back of her mind also, as she welcomed the raising of their own defences against the dark, was the knowledge that the same thing was happening in all the other houses in the street and the thought of it extended the sense of identification she had felt with the women at the party to all the people in them.

The crippled men shared in it and in the remembered wave of her compassion, for when she thought of them now crouching like everyone else in their own little lit oases in the dark, the pity she felt for them was stronger than the horror she had of their mutilated bodies.

She couldn't and didn't try to explain her feelings to herself. It was enough for her that somehow they lessened her horror of the crippled men; gave her some sort of defence against the feeling that her normal, everyday world might suddenly at any moment be transformed into the horrifying scene of her nightmare.

Yet still she could not quite rid herself of the creeping dread that this might happen—not while she was still caught up in the searching of the medical book; not while she could still hear the smothered sound of weeping in the night and feel herself smothering, too, in the hopelessness of her mother's grief.

4

The winter went by slowly that year, wet and cold and dark. She had forgotten how much dark there was in the winter time—or perhaps it was just because all the light and singing had gone out of the house that it seemed such a dark time to her. They went to bed early to save the light and there was no more singing with her mother out of the Redemption Song Book, no more listening to her father and laughing at him singing "Oh, Mister McGra, the Sergeant said" and "Biddie Mulligan, the pride of Kildrum." There was no Christmas at Grannie's that year. There probably wouldn't be any more Christmases at Grannie's, ever, her mother said. She couldn't afford all that horde of people descending on her nowadays.

The spring came and with it the impulse to run and shout in the pleasure of the sunlight and green growing freshness outside the house. But still, she found resentfully, although the burden of the dark days had dropped from her there was no escaping yet from the burden of her mother's grief. It still lived in the house with them like a ghost and her mother's haunted, stricken face was a constant reminder of its presence.

She tried of course; she could see how hard her mother was trying to be the same to them as she used to be, but the ghost was always there between her and her love for them. They themselves tried in their own way to show her how much they cared, by doing things that they thought would please her. But sometimes their plans misfired, like the time Nell said they should scrub the kitchen floor for her while she was out but they began to quarrel over the job and she came back to find the buckets of water overturned and everyone shouting with rage in the middle of the flooded floor.

They made plans for her birthday in April and each of them decided they would give her a specially good present that year. The Others began to save the pennies neighbours gave them for running errands and she helped William with the picture he had decided to draw, but she kept the plans for her own present to herself. It was violets she had in mind. Her mother was passionately fond of violets but none of the Others would have thought of trying to get some for her because they were never usually out in time for her birthday.

That spring, however, she had discovered a bank of them that nobody else knew about—not even Nell. It faced due south, right into the eye of the sun, and the flowers on it were further advanced than those in any other place. For weeks before her mother's birthday she had been making secret excursions to prospect it and as the date drew near she was satisfied that the violets would be fully out when she wanted them. She could hardly conceal her delight from the Others then for she knew her mother would like her present more than anything their money could buy. She managed to suppress her desire to boast, however, and with her secret still intact on the day before the birthday, set off by herself to pick the violets.

There were so many of them out by that time that the whole bank on which they grew glowed purple in the sunshine. It was a steep bank sloping upwards above the level of the field where Pearson of Castlemains pastured his lambing ewes. She checked cautiously that there was no one around before she climbed the gate, for though most of the ewes had dropped their young several months before she knew that she would still be chased for her life if the shepherd caught her in the lambing pasture. There was no sign of the shepherd however, and placing her hands on top of the wall that separated the field from the bank, she began to heave herself up.

It was a hard scramble as a rule to reach the bank for the wall was a high one. There was a dip on the far side of it, however, between it and the foot of the bank, and when she had pulled herself high enough to hook one leg over the wall a thrust with this leg and with her hands was usually enough to send her tumbling over and down into this shallow declivity. She managed it this time also and with her eyes screwed up tightly against the strain of the final thrust fell forward from the top of the wall.

She landed face down on something soft and wet and slippery that sent a pungent smell shooting up her nostrils. Her hands slithered over the wet softness as she levered herself up, opening her eyes as she did so. She was lying across a mound of something dirty-white and red. White of wool and red of blood—lambs' tails! The shepherd had been tailing the lambs and had thrown the tails over the wall and into the dip behind it. There was blood on her hands, her dress—gluey, sticky blood. Blood was stinking in her nostrils. Her face was smeared with blood.

She gasped, then screamed aloud with the horror of it and tried to push herself up and away from the bloody mess underneath her. Her hands could not reach far enough to find a grip beyond the mound of tails. Her knees when she tried to draw them up to lever herself upright could find no purchase on the soft mass so that she fell face down into it again. She writhed forward, her face slithering over the bloody tails and the gasps of revulsion choking back into her throat as she closed her lips tightly against the soft disgusting feel of them.

Her hands touched grass and closed on it, pulling her away from the horror of blood and dismemberment, giving her a grasp that enabled her to scramble upright, drop back down over the wall and run, run, run out of the field, down the lane running, running—oh dear God she could never run fast enough to get away from the feel of her face pushed down into the blood . . . into the blood and bits of bodies . . . blood from bits of bodies smeared over her nose, her eyes, her lips . . . she could smell the blood on her face, taste it . . .

She was still running when she was swung violently, suddenly, off her feet. The strong grasp of the hand that had caught her round her upper arm checked the wild sideways swing of her body and brought it back to crash against the dark bulk of the Castlemains shepherd planted in the path of her flight. His voice came rumbling at her with a spate of questions in the broad Scots dialect of the farm-workers. She tried to answer him but nothing except disjointed words and sobs came out of the chaos of horror in her mind, and in a sudden renewal of the wild impulse to run she began to try and struggle out of his grasp.

His other hand closed on her. He picked her up and turning about marched off down the lane carrying her against his chest. His jacket smelt of tobacco and sweat and sheep-dip. She heard the dull thud of his boots against the earth of the lane change to the sharp clack of metal heel plates on cobblestones; then she was swung down and found herself facing a door. The shepherd's hand came over her shoulder pushing the door open, and he steered her through it ahead of him.

There was a washhouse beyond the door. A big, broad-built woman stood in it with her arms up to the

156

elbows in a huge wooden tub of soapy water. She turned an astonished face on them and the shepherd said,

"Wash this bairn's face for her, Liz, and get some o' that muck off her dress. She's jist aboot daft in the heid wi' somethin' that happened tae her up by the lambin' field."

The big woman took a cloth off the edge of her wash-board. In silence she wiped the blood from her face and hands and legs with it and then sponged the front of her dress. The calm silence in which it was done was re-assuring and when the woman put the cloth down and asked quietly, "What happened ye then, ma hen?" she was able to answer sensibly,

"I was after the violets at the lambing pasture and I fell down on the lambs' tails *he* cut off."

"And ye got a fright. Ah weel, sma' wonder. And what were ye goin' tae dae wi' the violets, eh, ma hen? Gie them tae yer mammy?"

She nodded. "For her birthday," and the woman said, sympathetically, "Ach, puir bairn! Weel, never mind. Ye can aye get her some ither wee thing for a present."

The woman was kind, really kind like her own mother. It was a pity she had to sound rude.

"I don't want to. I don't care about a present now."

"Ach, ye'll think different aboot it the morn's morn. Sit ye doon there noo, and I'll fetch ye a drink o' milk and a bit scone. And you, my mannie, off ye go. The bairn'll be fine here."

The woman bustled through a door into the house and the shepherd, with a grin and a wink at her, went outside again. It was cold in the washhouse. She felt the gooseflesh rising on the damp skin of her arms and sat down on a stool that stood in one corner, crouching into herself and hugging her arms tightly over the wet front of her dress. She was shivering, shivering all over with cold and with a bitter ache of resentment against her mother for being the cause of all this.

The woman was kind but she didn't understand, she didn't know about the nightmares and the weeping in the night. It would be no use telling her that she didn't care about her mother now because she just couldn't bear any more horrifying things to happen. She was finished with her mother's grief now, finished with it. She wouldn't think about it ever again. She couldn't bear to think of it or the thing she had dreaded would come true again. The nightmare of the body in the churchyard would come smothering down on her in broad daylight like it had when her face had been pressed down into the blood and bits of bodies and she would scream and scream and scream till her head exploded in screaming . . .

She began to sob, shivering, choking sobs that brought the woman hurrying back into the washhouse. She had a glass of red liquid in her hand and she came briskly over to the stool with it.

"The glass o' milk was jist a tale to get Jock oot o' the

158

wey," she said comfortably, "or he'd hae hung aroond for some wine tae."

She held the glass out. "Drink it up noo. It's made frae elderberries and it's real guid."

The wine tasted hot and sweet with an after-bitterness that drew her lips together like the taste of an iron tonic. There was a warm glow in her chest after she had swallowed it.

"It was nice," she said appreciatively, and handed the glass back.

"Would ye like a wee drop mair? It'll pull ye thegether fine."

She nodded shyly. The woman disappeared again and came back with another glassful of wine. She drank it up quickly, feeling the glow spread farther inside her when it had gone down. The woman smiled at her and brought forward a damp-wrinkled hand holding a scone, split and spread thickly with butter.

"Away ye go then. Ye'll be fine noo, lass."

She found herself, scone in hand, being pushed gently to the door, thanking the woman still smiling down at her as she went. Then she was outside the door and crossing the cobbles of the farmyard with a spray of light, gay thoughts rising up into her mind from the pool of wine lying warm inside her. The thick butter rolled richly round her tongue as she bit into the scone. She swallowed luxuriously and broke into a skipping run down the lane. She was clean, clean, clean now of the blood and free, free at last of the dragging care for her mother! The words danced in her head to the time of her skipping steps and changed to the tune of one of her father's songs.

What's the news, what's the news, of my bold chevalier,
With his long-barrelled guns of the sea?
Say what wind from the south brings his messenger here,
With a hymn of the dawn for the free?

She began to sing it aloud, with a splendid vision of its tall golden hero in her mind. *"He is seven foot tall with some inches to spare,"* she sang, *"and his long golden hair hanging down,"* and saw him ahead of her in the sunshine as she sang—Kelly, the boy from Killarn, charging boldly up from the south to fight his lost brave battle for Ireland's freedom. And oh, he was a splendid man—and oh, how wonderful it was to have put all the blood and the horror and the nightmares away from her! How glad she was to be free of her mother's grief at last!

"I fell into the burn at Castlemains," she lied briefly later on at home when her mother challenged her draggled appearance, and felt no regret for the lie or shame at deceiving her mother. She felt nothing at all for her mother now, in fact, and when William and the Others produced their presents the next day, and her mother looked at her empty hands, she still felt nothing.

"I forgot." It was the simplest answer she could think of to her mother's questioning look, and when the ex-

160

pression on her mother's face changed to one of hurt disappointment she only offered a careless, "Sorry, Mam."

She wasn't used to lying and she could see her mother suspected there was something strange about her not having a present to give. She turned away but from the corner of her eye saw the hand that reached kindly out to her, and with an assumption of jauntiness she moved aside so that it could not touch her. The hand offered warmth and love, but you got nothing for nothing in this world. She had heard people say that often, and if she accepted the hand now she would have to give warmth and love in return. She would start caring again if she did that. She would be drawn back into the net of caring for her mother's grief and she couldn't bear that to happen again!

She ran out into the garden pretending not to hear the voice that called, "Bridie—come back, come back!" after her, and kept on running till she was out of earshot. She dropped to a walk then, moving slowly along, kicking a stone in front of her as she went and thinking about the time that had passed since her father died.

It was like a maze in her mind, a maze of dark and haunted places through which she had blundered looking desperately for a way out into the light again. Her mother's grief had lurked in the centre of all the dark and interlocking places in the maze, so that whichever way she turned she had been trapped with it. Until now!

Now she was free, she was back in the sunlight again, and there was nothing to remind her of all her terrified wanderings through the maze except the dull ache of longing for her father. She should have felt relieved, even triumphant as she had been the day before skipping home and singing "Kelly, the Boy from Killarn." But somehow she didn't. She only felt as she used to do when she had done something that had made her father angry with her—sad and guilty and lonely.

Very lonely.

5

The spring of the blood on the violets saw the beginning of a new pattern in all their lives for the last of the insurance money was finished round about this time and the Widow's Pension was all they had left to live on. "It can't be done," her mother told them. "Twenty-seven shillings a week for myself and the five of you—it just can't be done." They had to find money from somewhere or else go On the Parish.

Her mother looked for work in the village but there was nothing to be had there except rough scrubbing in the houses of the English people down by the sea. The rheumatism in her legs was too bad for that and so she answered advertisements in the Edinburgh paper till she got a job in a shop there. It meant she was away from home every day from early in the morning till the late evening, but Nell was thirteen by that time and so she managed to get an exemption from the school for her so that she could be at home to help in the house and cook the dinner for the rest of them.

Everything became suddenly, uncomfortably different without her mother at home through the day. They weren't used to looking after themselves and so they were always quarrelling with one another and with Nell —especially with Nell—over the jobs that had to be done. Nell was bossier than ever now that she was in charge but when her mother came home at night she had no time to listen to their complaints. She had no time for anything nowadays in the evenings, not even for tears. There was always so much preparing to do for the next day before she could get to bed and by that time she was too tired to bother about anything else.

"You'll just have to sort it out among yourselves," she told them wearily when they complained about Nell, and so they just had to put up with being bossed about —until the day, that was, when she had the bright idea of hitting back, not by resisting Nell, but by poking fun at her.

Nell could never bear to be laughed at so that all she had to do was to take the tune of "Shall We Gather at the River" from the Redemption Song Book and fit words to it that made the way she tried to boss them sound absolutely silly. It was a good marching tune and it was easy to persuade Moira and Aileen to join her in taunting Nell with the new words to it whenever she tried to bully them into doing something they didn't want to do. If it was a job like polishing spoons and pot lids they wanted to avoid they marched round the house singing the song at the top of their voices and beating out the time on the pot lids and when Nell rushed out to try and stop them they scattered laughing at the tears of helpless rage running down her cheeks.

It was too easy, really, she felt uncomfortably, and in spite of her dislike of being ordered about there were times when she felt oddly sorry for Nell. She couldn't help being bossy, after all, and even though they all knew very well she was only acting as usual she was still very much in earnest about being a Little Mother to the rest of them. The aftermath of shame at the cruelty in the joke she had started kept gnawing at her conscience until eventually she decided to offer a truce. When Nell accepted she was glad to drop the weapon of her ridicule and in this way, never agreeing but never quite breaking into open battle again, they managed to struggle on till the summer holidays came.

There were more changes for them all then. The travelling and the long day became too much for her mother and so she had to leave her job in Edinburgh and take what work she could find in the village. Without the good wages from the Edinburgh job the few shillings they earned at the little jobs they had done before—to teach them the value of money, her father said—suddenly assumed a new importance. They were real earnings now and luckily it was at this time that Mr. Purves decided to extend his round of paper deliveries. It was only Nell who had had a proper job with him till this time, with Aileen and herself doing the Sunday deliveries to give her a morning off. With all the new deliveries to make up, however, he needed Nell to help him in the shop now and so she and Aileen got to take over Nell's old route with the daily papers. Moira already had a job delivering milk from Denton's farm-lorry, and in addition to this all four of them were taken on that summer for the berry picking at Johnstone's fruit farm.

Their days were too full for quarrelling now—although the return of her mother's calm centre of authority to the house had made it die down in any case.

Each day started for them at six o'clock when they had to get up and ready to start the milk and paper rounds at half-past six. By eight o'clock they were all home having breakfast and they were down at the fruit farm by nine o'clock. This was an hour behind the time the rest of the pickers started work but Mr. Johnstone was so short of hands that he was glad, even, of latecomers. They were paid according to the weight they picked anyway, and so it was up to themselves to make up for the lost time.

"You're young and healthy," their mother told them. "Hard work won't hurt you," but it wasn't really hard work at the berries. It was only when it rained and they had to put on the long sacking aprons that the farmwomen called "brats" and crawl along the strawberry beds weeding as they went that their backs and knees ached. There weren't many days like that, however. Most of the time it was so hot that they had to wear bonnets to protect the backs of their necks from the sun.

The Others had all been at the berries before but this was her first experience of the work. She watched them carefully to begin with and found that Moira was the best picker. She pulled the berries from their stalks so quickly and neatly that she might have had eyes in the tips of her fingers, but it was no use watching her for as soon as she had filled as many baskets as she thought she should she disappeared on her own concerns.

"The rope has still to be made that will halter Moira," her father used to say, and it was true. Nobody could ever pin Moira down for long in the one place.

Nell was just as quick as Moira but she was very untidy and there were always leaves and stalks among the berries in her baskets. Aileen was much slower than the other two but she worked neatly and steadily and so, after the first day, she settled down into the pleasant rhythm of working on the opposite side of each bush from Aileen.

There was a great gang of other children from the village beside them at the berries so that there was always laughter and conversation flying back and forward along the rows of raspberry canes and between the thickets of currant bushes. And when the time came for turning in their day's pickings to be weighed and paid for there was more laughter in the good-natured scuffling that went on in the weighing house and in the excitement of feeling real wages in their hands.

They were allowed to eat their fill of the berries—except for the strawberries, of course, which were meant for the tables of the gentry—and each evening of these warm holidays she came home with her stomach full of sweet berries and her skin tingling richly with the day's sunshine. She stumbled sleepily to bed each night with the scent of ripe fruit still lingering in her nostrils, and as she fell asleep it was with remembered snatches of laughter echoing in her mind; and in her ears there was still a faint sound of the soothing bee-murmur that had hung all day around her in the hot, scented air of the fruit farm. It was still the mornings, however, when she was out delivering the papers to the big houses by the sea, that were the best part of the summer for her.

Everything was so fresh, so alive at that time of day that when she left the house in the morning it seemed to her that she was stepping out, not only into a new day, but into a new world. The colours of it were the rich colours of summer flowers—roses, hollyhocks, delphiniums, all glowing in a heraldic brilliance of red and gold and blue on the soft green field of their foliage. The essence of the perfumes the sun's first touch had drawn from their opening petals hung newly distilled on the air that she breathed, and as she ran along the street to the paper-shop the first chorale of small birds claiming ownership in the new day was still sounding loud and clear from all the gardens in the street.

Her way separated from Aileen's at the shop for they had split the round between them, Aileen taking the village and the farm-cottages and herself the big houses down by the sea. She rode alone each morning down the steep incline of the road to the sea, rode swiftly with delight in her speed on the message-bike towards an eastern arc of sky still suffused with the afterglow of sunrise. This was the road down which she had cycled once—a long time ago, howling aloud like an animal in the pain of her first realization of her father's death. But now, as she plunged swiftly each morning towards the saffron and rose and gold and green still glowing in the sky ahead of her she was caught up in a rush of exhilaration in which it seemed to her that she was flying, literally, gloriously flying, straight into the opalescent heart of this sunrise afterglow.

At the foot of the road were the houses of the English with their cars and cooks and nannies and children only seen in the summer holidays when they homed briefly from the mysterious world of English boarding schools. They were all asleep at this time, the rich English people and their pale-faced, alien children, sound asleep behind drawn curtains that cut them off from the morning world she had discovered. There was no one but herself there to see it; no one to come between herself and the live, springing freshness of their gardens at this hour. She could stand in any one of them and stare at a leaf, a petal, a silvered snail track, the pattern of a tree against the sky, until the impression of its colour and shape was so vividly imprinted on her mind that it became an integral part of her; until, sometimes, by some deeper magic of transference, the process was reversed and some part of herself was totally absorbed into the high point of glory on which the light and colour of the morning seemed momentarily to tremble.

Almost, at these moments, it seemed that Time stood still for her and she was painfully, breathlessly on the point of escaping from the closed circle of life and death in which she knew she was caught. But the feeling of identification with something outwith and beyond her normal consciousness was too fragile in concept to be sustained by the stumbling process of her thoughts. It touched her mind only lightly, and even as she struggled to understand, it would dissolve in her grasp and leave her with only a nameless yearning for something—she could not quite remember what it had been.

There were other, more easily understood pleasures on the morning paper round. She found nests at which she crouched watching the hen-birds stuffing food down the yellow gapes of their nestlings. Once she came on a group of weasels right in the middle of the road. They had formed themselves into a circle, and balancing upright on their hind legs were weaving their sinuous red-brown bodies back and forth, gravely, gracefully, like dancers engaged in some mysterious ritual. And once, as she stood by the high hedge of a garden sorting out her papers, a flight of swans appeared from the other side of it and flew so low over her head that for one thrilling moment the whole world was a gleam and a dazzle of smooth white bodies and a wild singing of great white wings around her head.

There were hazards also to be dealt with occasionally on the morning round. Some of the servants in the big houses were up and about, and though she rarely encountered any of them, there was Mr. Ferry, the big fat butler at "Fairview" who sometimes lay in wait for her and pretended to tickle her, and whom she feared for the strange gleam that came into his eyes when she could not escape from his pudgy hands running up and down her dress. There was Maggie Thomson, the maid at "The Villa" who screamed at her and called her "a child of sin" if she tracked any gravel over the white flagstones outside the kitchen door. And there were the dogs.

All the big houses kept dogs, all kinds and every size, and sometimes two or three to a house. Some of them were vicious and she had to keep a careful lookout in case any of these ones were loose when she arrived. She was not afraid of them, however, for her father had taught her how to deal with a vicious dog.

"Never turn your back on it," he had warned her. "Face up to it, stand perfectly still and speak commandingly, and nine times out of ten it will only snarl at you. There's always the tenth time, of course, when it might really attack and when that happens there's only one thing to do. Kick it in the teeth as hard as you can."

She had only to do this once—when Major Morrison's great black Alsatian appeared suddenly from round the corner of his house and sprang at her; and luckily that day she had on her heavy winter shoes instead of the sandals she usually wore, for it had rained through the night and the ground had still been very wet when she started on her round. The kick she aimed at it landed under the Alsatian's lower jaw, checking it in midleap and sending it squatting back on its haunches.

Now, when she had time to fully recognize the threat in its snarling muzzle, she *was* afraid, but what had worked once, she argued to herself, would work again. And anyway, she didn't dare turn her back on it to run away. She would have to wait now and see what happened.

She waited for the dog to come back to the attack but it only backed away and growled at her from a distance, and keeping her eye cautiously fixed on it, she edged towards the kitchen door with the papers. It opened unexpectedly as she reached it. Major Morrison stood there clutching a dressing gown round him and glaring down at her from under bushy pepper-and-salt eyebrows.

"Thought you were safe to kick the dog, eh?" he shouted. "But I saw you! I saw you—you—!"

"He sprang at me!" she blurted out, and from behind her a voice said, "That's right, sir. It was me let him oot the kitchen door this mornin' and he leaped straight for the lassie, but when I saw she kent hoo tae deal wi' him I just went on tae the shed for my kindlin' and didna bother."

172

It was fat Kirsty, the cook, coming out of the shed with a basket of kindling wood on her arm. She waddled up and put her bulk in between the two of them, talking all the time.

"He's vicious, Major, that's what he is. A' the message-laddies is feart o' him . . ."

A hand came out behind her back as she talked, flapping a signal to make off quietly. She took the chance the cook offered her and edged gradually away using the woman's broad back for cover. Piper, the black dog, growled again as she passed but he made no attempt at a further attack on her. She left the garden quickly without lingering, as she usually did, to look at Major Morrison's peach tree, and after she had delivered the paper the next day she would have left again as quickly if Kirsty had not waylaid her.

"Dinna you bother aboot that brute o' his, my hen," she told her comfortably, "for I'll keep him weel chained till ye're past, see? Away you now, if ye want tae, and hae anither look at that tree ye're aye gawkin' at. But nae touchin', see nae touchin'. The Major has every last yin o' thae peaches coonted."

She had counted them herself, many times, for she had watched them ripening all summer, but she would never have dreamed of taking any and she told Kirsty so earnestly as she thanked her for keeping Piper chained up. Then she went cautiously round to the south side of the house as usual, and stopped in front of the peach tree growing against the wall there.

She could never have enough of looking at Major Morrison's peaches. She had watched them from the time they had been small, yellowish-green globules on the stems, watched them draw sweetness and ripeness from the summer till their skins were golden yellow flushed deeply with a rich dusky pink and overlaid with a barely perceptible fuzz of minute hairs glinting in the sun. And now that they were full ripe it seemed to her that she was looking at summer itself hanging heavy on the stalk. If she reached out a hand she could touch it. A hand closed over one of these peaches would feel the whole ripe sweet warmth of summer enclosed within it.

"Nae touchin'," Kirsty had said, *"Nae touchin',"* but what she had meant, of course, was "no stealing" and so it had been no lie to say that she wouldn't dream of touching the peaches. Just holding the fruit in her hand was different. That was no crime, no crime at all.

The palm of her right hand was tingling already in anticipation and she felt it rising from her side as if it was being drawn magnetically towards the fruit. When it was only inches away from one of the peaches she stopped it with a tremendous exertion of will. It must be of her own accord, knowingly, that she touched the peach, for only then would she be able to say truly to herself,

"I reached out my hand and took hold of summer."

Deliberately she advanced her hand and closed it over a peach, very lightly, very gently, letting the ripe

174

round fruit nestle in her palm. The skin was smooth, not slippery-smooth like an apple but soft-smooth like velvet. The sun had warmed it. The peach was a big one. It filled her hand. Her hand was full of sun and ripeness. She closed her eyes and withdrew her mind from everything else except her hand and the warm, heavy ripeness within it. Now she was holding summer in her hand!

Gently, still very gently, with eyes opened again to control the disengaging of her fingers, she released the peach. She backed from the tree a little fearful that her touch might have weakened its hold on the stalk but the peach did not fall, and with a long breath of satisfaction and relief she ran off down the drive to her bicycle.

She went back to the peach tree as usual the next morning but to her disappointment, most of the fruit had been picked. Kirsty's voice hailing her sounded as she turned away from it and she went slowly back towards the kitchen door. The cook met her halfway.

"I was ower late tae catch ye afore ye went roond the hoose," she began in an agitated voice, "but I'm warnin' ye noo, hen, keep away frae that damned peach tree. The Major'll skin ye alive if he catches ye near it noo."

"What for?" It was hard to keep the laugh out of her voice. Kirsty looked so comical when she was flustered.

"Because his peaches was pinched last night—that's what for!" Kirsty snapped. "And ye can wipe that damn

175

silly grin off your face for it's you, he says, that did it!"

"*Me!*"

"Aye, you. When he found the tree stripped he asked me did I ever see you near it, and what could I say then? Dammit lassie, I ken ye meant nae harm jist lookin' but I couldna sin my soul by sayin' I hadna seen ye there, could I?"

"But I never, I never! I didn't steal his peaches!" she protested wildly, but Kirsty only said urgently,

"Get your road oot o' here then. The Major's fizzin' mad. Away afore he catches ye!" and waddled rapidly back to her kitchen.

She finished her round that morning more annoyed than alarmed at Kirsty's warning. He had an awful cheek, the old Major, saying that *she* had stolen his peaches! It was very likely Billy Carstairs had done it— he was a one for stealing from all the gardens! Everybody knew that so why should she get the blame?

She was so taken up with her indignation that she had no eyes for any of the usual attractions on her round that morning. It was a long time, however, between seven o'clock in the morning and lousing-time at the berries, and by the time that the whistle blew to call the pickers into the weighing house the Major and his stolen peaches had slipped away to the back of her mind. She had told the Others about it at the berries but now she even forgot to mention it to her mother at suppertime, and when the message came that Mr. Purves wanted her at the shop she ran along without a thought of Major Morrison in her mind.

Mrs. Purves was at the counter in the front shop. She jerked her head at the door into the back shop and said briefly,

"In there. Both of them."

The words made no sense to her. "Who's both of them?" she asked in bewilderment, but Mrs. Purves only said without looking at her, "In you go, Bridie," and she went slowly through to the back shop.

Mr. Purves was there with Major Morrison. They were both red in the face as if they had been arguing about something. Major Morrison scowled when she came in and Mr. Purves said quietly,

"Major Morrison has been telling me something about you, Bridie. He says he suspects you of having stolen peaches from his garden. Is that true?"

"No, it isn't," she said promptly. "I never did. Never!"

Mr. Purves turned away from her and said to Major Morrison, "That's good enough for me, sir. You'll have to look elsewhere for your thief."

"Dammit man, are you going to take that brat's unsupported word?" the Major shouted. "I know for a fact that she's been hanging around that peach tree all summer. And she's a McShane, isn't she?"

"Aye, she's a McShane." Mr. Purves was still very quiet but the Major continued to shout.

"Well then, what d'you expect? The father was a bloody Red, wasn't he, and fellows like him have no respect for other people's property. The kid's bound to be tarred with the same brush—probably lying her head off!"

"McShane's politics were his own affair," Mr. Purves said coldly. "But I can tell you one thing and that is that a lie was anathema to him and he brought up his bairns to think the same way."

"*Anathema!*" the attraction of the new word was too strong to resist and quickly she pounced in before anyone else could speak.

"What's 'anathema' please, Mr. Purves?"

He gave her an exasperated look but explained patiently enough, "It means something you can't stand at any price."

"Thank you, Mr. Purves." She turned to the Major and said with dignity, "It's perfectly true what he says, and a lie is anathema to me too, and I *didn't* steal your peaches. And anyway, my dad wasn't a bloody Red like you said. He was a revolutionary, like Christ."

Mr. Purves coughed behind his hand. The Major stared at her with his face turning from fiery red to a peculiar purple shade. His pepper-and-salt eyebrows worked up and down and he began to gasp and splutter as if he had lost his breath. As she shrank back in alarm from the effect her words seemed to have had on him he roared,

"Dammit Purves, this is *too* much! She maltreats my dog, she steals my fruit, and now she stands and spouts at me like a bloody street-corner agitator! It's too much, man! I won't have her coming near my

178

house again—you'll have to get rid of her!"

"Look sir," Mr. Purves said, suddenly stern and as loud as the Major, "we've been into the question of the dog and you know as well as I do that he's vicious. All the delivery boys in the village can testify to that too, so let's keep the dog out of it. As for the fruit, I know this child is truthful and completely honest, and furthermore, I think it's very bad taste to drag her father's politics into the affair."

"I'd remind you, Purves, that you're talking to a commissioned officer in His Majesty's Forces!" The Major nearly choked on the words he was so angry now, but Mr. Purves didn't even blink. He drew himself up as straight as his wooden leg would allow and saluted smartly.

"Sir!" His hand dropped down, but he continued to hold himself erect. "We're both retired now, Major," he said softly. "The war's over for both Sergeant Purves and Major Morrison now—but I'm beginning to feel there was a lot of truth in the gospel of that other war poor Pat McShane preached so hard."

"You decline to make any further investigation into my complaint then?"

"I do, sir. Do you wish me to cancel your paper order?"

The Major glared. "You're a bloody Red too!" he shouted, and stamped out of the back shop, slamming the door behind him.

Mr. Purves sighed and rubbed his hand over his face;

then he lowered himself stiffly into his chair. "He couldn't cancel the order, anyway," he said to the opposite wall. "Nowhere else *but* here to get his papers."

She stood uneasily waiting to be told to go but Mr. Purves kept staring at the wall. At last he turned his eyes on her. He beckoned her closer and when she was standing in front of him he said,

"Keep your mouth shut about your Dad's ideas, Bridie. They don't go down well in the village—not with *his* sort running things."

"I know," she said wisely. "The Tories don't want the working classes to live decent lives."

"Oh God, Bridie!" Mr. Purves groaned. "You're Patrick McShane's daughter all right—you just won't take a telling, will you! You'll live to be hung, so you will, my girl."

She opened her mouth to protest but Mr. Purves cut in before her. "And another thing, young shaver, you think too much and you see too much and it's all there in your face. It's not natural, Bridie, not the thing at all for anyone your age to be sizing people up the way you do. Grown-ups don't like it—my God, did you not see the Major's face when you were standing there reading him through and through with your eyes for the pompous, prejudiced old goat that he is!"

"I'm sorry, Mr. Purves," she said humbly. "It's just that I like thinking about things and I can't help watching people. It's very interesting, you know."

Mr. Purves stared up at her face and then with a

180

shake of his head at her, "Lassie, lassie," he said slowly, "you'll have a hard row to hoe in this life."

He struggled up from his chair holding on to her shoulder for support, and when he was on his feet he said, "Think if you must, Bridie, but keep your thoughts to yourself. And watch the expressions on that face of yours. Remember, there's nobody likes to be seen as they really are—especially not when it's a shrimp like you that's doing the seeing! Go on, now."

He pushed her to the door and she went obediently, but with her hand on the handle she paused and turned.

"Mr. Purves . . ."

"Imphm?"

"That was fine—the way you stood up for my father."

"You stood up not so bad yourself, lassie."

She nodded, smiling at him with a sudden feeling of comradeship, and smiling back at her he quoted,

"Up the Rebels . . ."

She could not resist the invitation and in a fair imitation of the Irish in her father's voice she finished the quotation,

". . . and to hell with poverty!"

They both burst out laughing and she went through the front shop on the crest of their laughter leaving Mrs. Purves looking after her with an astonished expression on her face.

6

Mr. Purves' lecture was a revelation to Bridie in some ways for it had never occurred to her before that there was anything actually wrong in the interesting business of observing people, any more than there was in observing things. Now, she could see, she would have to be very careful to hide her habit of slipping in through all the cracks she had discovered in the solid wall of the grown-up world and noting all the interesting differences between the people there. It was not only wrong, apparently. It was dangerous also, if they guessed what she was thinking about them. Look at how angry the old Major had got!

She would have to learn to hide this enquiring, observant part of her mind, the part that did all the thinking for her, she decided, and gradually she worked out how it could be done.

She began to laugh louder, talk faster, caper even more energetically than was usual for her when she was in the company of adults now. At first, it was only nervousness that made her do it, but when she discovered that the exaggeration of her normal activity and talkativeness made people treat her as if she was only an empty-headed chatterbox, she realized that this was all the concealment she needed for her passionate interest in things and people.

It meant that she had to learn to think in two different ways at the same time, of course. In fact, it was almost like being two separate people. On the surface she was a wilder version of the Bridie everyone still expected her to be, so full of energy that she never walked where she could run, the noisy one among the McShanes who was always laughing and talking nineteen to the dozen. Underneath this there was the other part of her mind, like another person watching all her antics and observing the effect they had.

It was slightly contemptuous of the ease with which they diverted adult attention from itself, but it was lonely there in hiding. *She* was lonely in fact, for this was a part of herself she could not show to other people or share with them—at first, because she was afraid to let anyone know of it, and later, when the habit of thinking on two levels had become established, because it seemed to her that people would think it odd and silly of her to be like this.

There were two grown-ups, however, with whom she never felt any need to pretend or to hide this other, thinking, part of herself. Mr. Miller, the President of the Literary Society, who lent her books from his library was one of them, and Mr. Gladsmuir was the other. People said Mr. Miller was dotty because he never did anything but read—he even walked down the street with his nose in a book—but she didn't think he was dotty. He let her take any book she wanted from his library and every time she went in he would discuss the book he was reading himself the way he used to discuss books with her father, talking all the time as if she was the same age as himself. Sometimes she didn't understand properly all that he said, but it was very interesting all the same and not dotty at all.

Mr. Gladsmuir still had wrong ideas about Christ of course, but he still wasn't like other people for he never thought it odd or comical as they did if he heard her declaiming aloud something like,

"O ye daughters of Jerusalem, weep over Saul who clothed you in scarlet and other delights . . ."

He would stop and talk to her and agree it was a peachy bit, the one about the mountains of Gilboa and the shield of Saul being vilely cast away, and he never seemed to mind her looking at him and thinking that he was really quite poor although he was a minister, or noticing the pleasure he took in the singing sound of the words when he quoted a bit of the Bible himself.

Mrs. Mackie, the headmistress, saw through her easily, of course. Those sharp grey eyes of hers missed nothing that went on in either of her classes—and in any case, when she went up to the first of them after the summer holidays that year and got to write the

184

kind of essays she wanted to, she found she couldn't do them properly without giving away some of her private, underneath way of thinking.

Mrs. Mackie was too much taken up with Aileen that year, however, to bother much about her. Aileen was in the class ahead of her, the top class that would have to pass the Qualifying Examination before they went up to the George Wishart Secondary Institute at the beginning of the next school year, and she was certain to win the Dux Medal for the school. Moira had won it the year before, but Aileen was a genius, Mrs. Mackie said; she would sweep the boards of all the other prizes as well.

There was the Menzies Memorial Prize for Arithmetic and the Nelson Trophy and the Tait Prize for English and usually they went to different pupils, but Mrs. Mackie was right for Aileen did win them all that year on top of the Dux Medal. Then it was her turn to be one of the Big Ones in the top class and Mrs. Mackie began to lecture her about working hard and keeping the medal in the family.

"You're the fourth McShane I've put through my hands, Bridie," she told her. "Nell was quick and intelligent but she was very erratic. She lacked concentration. Moira was shrewd, very shrewd, but she was also stubborn and would only work at what pleased her. Aileen—" she paused, and her face took on a faraway, dreamy look; then she shook her head and went on briskly, "Well, of course, none of you can expect to cut such a swathe academically as Aileen will. But you can and you should win the Dux Medal for your family again *if* you will stop dreaming. You must come down to earth, my child, and try to realize that there are other subjects in the examination apart from the English essay."

She listened mutely to the lecture, nodding her head at all the right places though all she was doing was admiring the beautifully precise way Mrs. Mackie spoke. At the end of it she said, "Yes, miss. Thank you, miss," as she was expected to do, and promptly put the examination out of her mind. She wasn't interested in the Dux Medal anyway. Jean Bailey could have it if she wanted to—and she did, of course, she was always swotting away at something!

There were other and much more exciting things to do than swotting for exams, now that she was one of the Big Ones! They made the rules in the playground and the younger children had to do what they said, but she was the best in the school at inventing new games and so it was her lead they followed. Even the people in her own class joined in when they saw what fun the rest of them were having but the games were her invention and so they had to abide by her rules too. It was easy to make them all do what she wanted. She began to understand why it was that Nell liked being the boss, but the attraction of imposing her will on the other children never lasted for long after she discov-

186

ered one day how much more exciting it was to hold their attention by talking.

She was sitting with three other girls at the top of the steps leading to the front door of the school when it happened. They could hear Mrs. Mackie's cairn terrier puppy howling from the shed in the schoolhouse garden and they were all feeling sorry for him because he had been locked in there for romping about in the sitting room and breaking one of Mrs. Mackie's fine glass ornaments.

"He didn't know it was a *good* ornament," one of the girls said indignantly, and the girl sitting beside her said,

"Oh well, a widow woman like her with neither chick nor child of her own—you couldn't expect *her* to have much understanding of young things."

It gave them a very grown-up feeling to talk like this now that they were all eleven and so they agreed wisely with her without letting on that they knew she was only quoting something she had heard her mother say.

From talking of the cairn puppy they went on to talk of other dogs in the village and Bridie told them about the various big dogs in the houses on her paper round. She had gone on to the story of how Piper had attacked her the previous summer when she noticed that another group of girls sitting on a lower step had turned round to listen. She began to embroider on the tale, bringing in Kirsty and the Major, and other chil-

187

dren attracted by the laughter she raised began drifting nearer to the steps.

More and more of them gathered until she had half the school grouped round her, and as she had to raise her voice to enable those on the outskirts to hear it, so did the thrill of holding an audience captive spur her on to add more and more imaginary detail until in the end she was building an entire new tale of her own devising out of the original one. The bell to mark the end of the dinner-hour sounded as she came to the end of her story and in the scramble to form the lines for marching into class several voices called out to her,

"Tell us another one tomorrow, Bridie!"

She promised recklessly without having any idea of what she was going to say, but when dinnertime came the next day it was easy after all. All she had to do was to start talking and the story spun itself. Once she was launched on it the first hard core of her listeners gathered more and more of the playing children around it until she was the centre of all their listening faces again. But this time the bell went before she had finished for she had deliberately spun the story out, as much for her own pleasure in telling it as for the thrill of holding an audience with it. The following day, by request, she went on telling the next part of the story, and that was the beginning of what Mrs. Mackie called her "lunch-time serials."

The teachers all got to hear about it, of course. They knew everything that went on in the school and eventually Mrs. Mackie asked her, "Have you ever tried to write any of your stories down, Bridie?"

It was on the tip of her tongue then to tell her about "The Man with a View of Heaven," but the shoe box with all her scribbled sheets in it had been left to gather dust in the box-room because she hadn't wanted to go on with it after her father died. It would never be a book now. None of her stories would ever be a book. They were just for the fun of making them up and telling them, for the thing she really wanted to write now was poetry. She had known that ever since she had had the chance to read the poetry books that were issued to Mrs. Mackie's classes and had discovered that the poems in them were different from the baby stuff they had been given to read in the lower classes.

These were real poems they got to read nowadays, poems that sang with lines like, "the shallow sea, the spring-time sea of green." And now poetry was her love for it had opened out like a light in her mind the knowledge that *this* was the thing she had been groping after in the essays Miss Dunstan had so cruelly red-pencilled. It was harmonious cadences of sound such as this she had wanted to create then. It was just such a smooth and colourful mosaic of words as the one in these poems that she had been trying to fit together when she picked and chose so carefully over the ones in her own small store.

But more than that she had discovered, and that was that poetry could express ideas in a form that made

189

every other way seem incredibly roundabout and clumsy. In a few lines a poem could say something that took hours and hours of complicated thinking for her to work out, and say it so exactly, moreover that—

"Bridie!" Mrs. Mackie's voice came sharply in her ear. "I am still waiting for an answer, Bridie."

She came back with a start to the classroom and saw that the rest of the class were waiting too. Their eyes were all on her, full of curiosity—and something else. What was it? What was it their eyes said? What *would* they say if she told Mrs. Mackie,

"No, I don't want to write stories. I want to be a poet."

They would laugh! The laughter would come into their eyes and then they would laugh aloud at her, Class Seven and Class Six as well would split their sides at the idea of Bridie McShane the poet!

Her heart began to beat very hard and her hands shook so much that she had to look down and clasp them hard together under the desk, but Mrs. Mackie said very gently,

"There's no need to look so upset, Bridie. I'm not going to eat you!" and she realized instinctively that the question would not be pressed any further.

She raised her head and said humbly, "No, miss. I'm sorry, miss." And in a rush of gratitude for the relief from questioning added the lie, "I expect I will—write stories one day, I mean. I quite like it."

"Good. We have an author in our top class this year,

then. Now, let us see what all the others are going to be when they grow up. Janette—what about you?"

The questioning went on right round all the others in the class after Janette said she wanted to be a nurse and Mrs. Mackie didn't bother her any more except when Jean Bailey said she wanted to be an accountant and Mrs. Mackie said that was quite right and proper because she was good at Arithmetic and worked hard at it—not like Bridie McShane who would fail the Arithmetic part of the exam if she didn't pay a little more attention to the subject.

That was just to frighten her to work harder at it, of course, because she wasn't all that bad at Arithmetic, and she still didn't care when Jean Bailey won the Dux Medal and she only came second because she still won all the English prizes, which was what she wanted to do. And by that time, in any case, she had taken the plunge and started to write her own poetry and that was the only thing that mattered to her in her last term at the village school.

It was much harder to do than she had thought it would be. Quite a short poem took her weeks to write and even then she wasn't sure if it was any good or whether it was just certain lines and phrases in it that had caught the idea in her mind. There was no one except Mr. Miller she could ask for advice on the proper way to do it but she was shy of telling even him that she wanted to be a poet. It was nearly time for the summer holidays to start that year before she could pluck up enough courage to take the exercise book with her poems in it down to his house one evening when she went to change her books for others in his library.

He was sitting at his desk reading when she came in and he started to talk right away—"Listen to this, Bridie. An interesting, a most interesting commentary on Redmains Castle I've turned up out of *Domestic and Castellated Architecture in Scotland*. There would appear to have been even more than the usual Scottish baronial predilection to homicide in the Redmains family—"

He began to read from a big black-bound volume on the desk in front of him and she listened for several minutes without really taking in what he was saying. Then quietly she slid the exercise book across the desk to rest beside the book about Redmains.

"What's this? Eh? What's this you have here?"

He glanced aside from his book and poked her exercise book with his forefinger, pushing it away from him.

"It's poetry," she muttered. "Mine. I wrote it."

"*You* wrote it?" He shot a look at her and another at her book, then his eyes came back to her. He pushed his spectacles up on to his forehead and, staring at her as if he had never seen her before, he said in a surprised voice,

"Good gracious, child, how you've grown! How old are you now, eh?"

"I'm just going on twelve," she told him.

"Twelve, eh? Well, well. Time passes, my child, time

passes. You were hardly as tall as this desk the first time your father brought you here with him!"

She could remember that, the first time she had felt books all round her and listened to the voices of her father and Mr. Miller rumbling deeply over her head. Her father had never thought Mr. Miller was dotty and it struck her suddenly then that perhaps it was because he missed the discussions the two of them used to have that he had kept on lending her books and talking to her about them after her father died.

He had her exercise book open in his hand now, peering intently at it through his spectacles pushed right down on to the tip of his nose.

"You're very fond of assonance," he said, stabbing at a page with his finger.

She wasn't sure of the meaning of the word but she was too wise in Mr. Miller's ways to ask. She took the Oxford Dictionary down from its shelf instead and started to look for "assonance." As always, she found so many other interesting words she had never seen before that she carried on reading the dictionary until the sudden sound of his voice startled her attention back to Mr. Miller again.

"Well, my dear, they're crude, very crude," he was saying, "and naturally, they're rather derivative. There is a certain felicity in the phrasing, however. Yes, a certain felicity. One detects the workings of an original mind here and there."

He read over a page or two again, muttering and

nodding to himself, then he put the book down on his desk and walked over to the window. She watched him standing there looking out into the garden and jingling the loose change in his pockets, but he was silent so long that she began to think he had forgotten she was there. At last, without turning round, he said,

"There's a curious thread runs through these attempts of yours—curious, that is, for a person of your age. It reminds me of something—I can't think . . . I can't think . . ."

He muttered to himself again and then suddenly, "Wait! I've got it!" he exclaimed, swinging round from the window and reaching up to a volume on one of the shelves. He flicked it open and ran a finger down one of the pages. "There's a couple of lines from Andrew Marvell here—ah yes. Here it is—

"*'But at my back I always hear,*

"*'Time's wingèd chariot hurrying near.'*

"Now here, you see, the poet has compressed into—"

She interrupted him, crying out breathlessly, *"But that's it!* That's the idea I've had ever since—that's what I've been *trying* to say all along!"

He closed the book, put it carefully back on the shelf, sat down at his desk and polished his spectacles carefully. He fixed them firmly back on his nose, stared hard at her through them, and then he asked quietly,

"Ever since when, Bridie?"

"Since Bluey died."

"Bluey? Bluey? Talk sense, child. Who or what was Bluey?"

"Nell's rabbit," she explained. "He died, and we were having a funeral for him. William didn't understand what dead was and I tried to explain it to him—"

She went on to tell him about everything that had happened to her in the lane that day she had run away from Bluey's funeral—the shock of understanding what death really was and of realizing that it would happen to her; the fear she had had ever since underneath all her pleasure in being alive of Time pursuing her—the fear of the final moment when it would catch up with her and she would die as her father had done. It was an overwhelming relief to be able to speak about it at last to someone who understood what she was talking about, so overwhelming that she quite forgot her manners to a grown-up and hushed Mr. Miller down on the one occasion he tried to interrupt her.

"I hadn't realized," he said when she had finished at last. "I'm sorry, my child, I hadn't realized that you missed your father so acutely. I'm afraid the experience has forced some aspects of your development more than is natural—or indeed, advisable—at your age."

The last part of it sounded like a rebuke to her. She flushed under the words but took heart again when he added kindly, "However, I have no doubt this morbid phase will pass. You'll see, my dear, you will view all this in a very different light when you are older.

You'll grow out of it, find wider horizons, different interests. The loss of a loved parent after all, tragic though it may be in childhood, assumes different meanings when one is grown-up."

He went on talking but the words went over her head for she was too absorbed in the idea he had just put forward to listen to him. It had simply never occurred to her before that all these things would automatically cease to bother her one day, but it did make sense, now that she thought of it. It had all started with her father dying, after all, and it was thinking about him, missing him so much that kept the fear of Time catching up with her, of dying, always active in her mind.

Growing up was *bound* to make a difference to all that. Grown-ups didn't need their fathers the way children did, after all, so there was bound to come a time when she wouldn't miss hers anymore—when she would forget all about him, in fact, and all the things connected with him. It changed the whole problem for her, she thought exultantly, made it just a matter of waiting for the day when she would be grown-up and could think differently about everything. She could look forward to that now when she was afraid, deep down under all her thoughts, of Time catching up with her.

It would be a long time, of course, before she was grown-up. She realized that, but she didn't really mind how long the waiting time was now that she knew there was this refuge waiting for her at the end of it. She was glad, truly and marvellously glad that she had told Mr. Miller all about it and she would have liked to thank him for his explanation, but he was still talking and she didn't like to interrupt him.

It was the technicalities of writing poetry he was holding forth on now, she discovered as she began to listen to him again, and what he had to say was so interesting that the first part of their conversation gradually retreated into the background of her mind. When she went home eventually, it was still without having thanked him, but she had the book he had quoted from under her arm and a whole lot of new words like "pentameter" and "strophe" carefully stored in her mind.

She was warm with satisfaction too over the way he had received the confession of her desire to be a poet. He hadn't seen anything at all foolish in it. In fact, it had been quite clear that he had thought it a good idea because, he had told her, poetry was the most satisfying of all the arts. And then, with a wry little smile, he had added,

"But the least lucrative, I fear!"

Which proved that he wasn't dotty at all because that was the only drawback she herself could see to being a poet. There wasn't much money in it, and money, of course, was still the chief problem in her family, the problem around which everything else in their lives was centred.

7

Ever since her father had died, it seemed to her, their daily life where money was concerned had been like a perpetual crossing from bank to bank of a dangerous, turbulent river. The banks of the river were Fridays, the day on which her mother drew the Widow's Pension and they knew they could rest easy with the rent paid and the groceries bought for the weekend. The days from Sunday onwards were the slippery stepping-stones on which they recrossed the torrent, balancing from one to the other with the help of money grubbed from here, there and anywhere till Friday, the opposite bank, was reached again.

The few shillings they earned from their various jobs and the money brought in by berry picking in the summer had to be put aside for buying them shoes and other things her mother couldn't make down or make over from the cast-offs that were handed to her or that she bought at jumble sales. Otherwise, she had to do the balancing for all of them with her earnings from

198

casual scrubbing jobs or the bit of fine sewing that sometimes came her way.

In the summer time too they took in lodgers, all the rest of the family crowding into the kitchen to sleep while the two upper rooms were let, so that there was more to eat and less worry at this time of the year. It was the winter time that was bad, but even in the winter they managed without Going On the Parish which was a thing her mother was determined not to do because, "Your father would turn in his grave," she told them.

For some time she had believed this would literally happen if they went On the Parish and had sat in agonies of suspense every time the dreaded point was reached when they had to discuss how they were going to manage without that last appeal to the Parish. By that twelfth summer, however, when she started to think of the money problem in relation to her future as well as to the present of all of them, she was old enough to have put such babyish imaginings behind her; to see instead the reality of their poverty and to realize also the changes it had wrought in her mother.

She was a different person now from the wild, grief-stricken figure of the first months after her father's death, but she was different too from the other Mammy —the one she could only remember now as a gentle voice, a warm presence, a kind, smiling face framed in a cloud of soft, dark hair. The gentleness, the kindness were still there in her face but now the features of it were perpetually drawn with strain and there were always dark smudges of worry bruising the skin below her eyes.

The dark hair that had once curled softly round her face was straight as a poker now for there was no money to spare for perms, and though she tried to frizz it out with tongs, sometimes, the curl was always taken out of it again by the steam of the hot water in all her scrubbing and dishwashing jobs. It all made her seem very plain and old-looking, especially since she never wore anything nowadays but that old black dress— the one that had been bought for the funeral—in the summer with the sleeves rolled up and the neck turned in for coolness and in the winter with a cardigan over it. It was only because she had no money to buy another dress that her mother always wore this one, of course, but this was something she knew without really realizing it till that twelfth summer of hers.

The MacGowans from Glasgow were their holiday lodgers that year. Mrs. MacGowan had a new holiday outfit of red-and-white printed silk and suddenly one day when she noticed her mother staring at it she realized that the look in her eyes was one of envious, hungry longing. Quickly, with a rush of embarrassed pity for her mother and an odd feeling of guilt on her own part, she averted her eyes from the two women, Mrs. MacGowan so smart and holiday-fied in her gay silk dress and her mother so drab and poor-looking in her dusty black with its shabby little cover-up of faded print apron. She just hadn't realized. She had got so used to it—

She went out of the kitchen with justifications and excuses jostling for a hearing in her mind and with shame growing through them at the thought of the way *they* had all complained of wearing jumble-sale dresses and handed-down coats. And with shame too she remembered other things—such as the way they used to grumble at getting up to go to work on cold winter mornings even though they knew how badly the money they earned was needed.

All the time the MacGowans stayed with them that look of her mother's kept recurring to her, and the ripples of all it implied spread farther and farther out in her mind; the way her mother had worked to keep them all, never complaining of the long hours she spent stooped over piles of dirty dishes in other people's sinks or of the rheumatics in her knees that made her limp so badly when she had spent a long time on her knees at a scrubbing job. How brave she was, never complaining of the pain that kneeling gave her or of the way the soda in the scrubbing water roughened the skin of her hands till it broke and bled. And how still, in spite of all she had done for them, she had found strength to fight other people's battles as well—for God was still in her life, she hadn't really meant it that terrible day she had cried out, *"There's no God!"*

She still lived the way it said you should in the

Bible, loving your enemies and not hating them that despise you—hadn't she stood between the Matheson children and their father all these terrible times he had got drunk and wanted to belt them about? Hadn't she been the only one in the village to stand up beside Willie and Alec Grant when they got converted by the Faith Mission Sisters and the whole village had turned out to jeer at them preaching from the Market Cross? They had brought rotten eggs and stones to pelt the Grant boys with that night but when her mother stood up beside them and cried, *"Who throws a stone at Christ's work, throws it at Christ!"* they were all ashamed and they even gave Willie Grant a presentation watch when he went off to be a missionary in Africa.

As one incident after another flooded in through the newly opened door in her mind, the growth of the guilt she felt for her former blindness was accompanied by another feeling—the realization that she was seeing her mother for the first time not just as her mother but as a person in her own right. And this shabby, drawn-faced woman, she saw now from the depths of her shame, this woman who for all she never had a new dress to her back and uncomplainingly did the lowest, most menial work in the village, was still a person of great dignity and courage.

She was proud of her! She wanted to run to her and tell her *how* proud she was to have her for her mam, how much she really loved her in spite of having turned away from her that day in the spring of the blood on the violets, but she had got out of the way of running to tell her anything since then. She couldn't even begin to think how she would say such things to her mother. It would be like talking to a stranger, and all through her own fault too for it was she who had repulsed her mother, not her mother who had turned from her.

Her mother still loved her. She knew that as certainly as she knew now that she would have to die someday, and the realization of how deeply she must have hurt her that spring brought with it an overwhelming feeling of guilt. Nor was there the solace for this that she had discovered for other feelings, of weaving a poem about it, for there was nothing beautiful or dramatic about guilt. It was just a shabby, dirty thing she had to carry around with her till she could find some way of confessing it to her mother. But how? How did you ask pardon of someone you scarcely knew—how confess love to a stranger?

The MacGowans' holiday came to an end. Mrs. MacGowan departed with her red-and-white silk dress but the reminder of it stayed like a maggot at the heart of the warm sweet days of the berry-picking season, like a shadow laid across the shining heraldic colors of her secret morning world.

That summer was very still and hot. They stayed awake late upstairs, not sleeping because of the stuffiness of the room. And sometimes, when one or other of them would slip out of bed and pad across to the window to kneel and suck in what freshness there was in the air outside, the rest would follow and they would crouch together looking out across the dark gap of the Firth to the golden necklace of lights strung out along the shore of Fife on the other side of the water.

"*A beggar's mantle fringed with gold.*" That was what Fife was called in the geography book at school because the coast was rich and the inland area was poor. But that wasn't the real reason, not the real reason at all, she thought on all those stifling nights they stared out over the darkness of the Firth. It was because the lights twinkling round the coast were a golden fringe on the dark and ragged outlines of the land on hot summer nights; because the hills of Fife were like the dark, humpy figures of bent old beggarmen, too old and poor and blind to look behind them and see the soft glory of gold that night had swirled suddenly on to the trailing hems of their rags.

Nearer at hand, too, lights twinkled late in the big houses down by the sea, lights for the dinner parties the English people gave, with silver and fine china and wine red or gold in frail, silvery tulips of glass. Her mother had told them what the dinner parties were like for she often got a job at them, helping with the washing up. It meant being up very late and all the standing hurt her feet when she had already been on them all day, but if they divided out the work that still had to be done between them when they came home from the berries she managed to get enough rest beforehand to be able to stick it out till the job was finished.

That was how it was that night, the sweltering hot night that summer when rich, red-faced Mrs. Benson gave her dinner party. Her mother went out to a job there after her rest and they all got on with the work she had left for them to do. The house was stuffy, even though every window was open and when William asked her to help him with the woodchopping and the coal-carrying for the next day's fire she was glad to escape into the garden with him.

William chattered all the time they worked, telling her of another of his schemes for making money. He was always trying to think of ways of Getting Rich, as he called it, and it sounded funny coming from such a little boy. The Others laughed at his schemes but she always kept a straight face because she knew William was easily hurt. This time, however, she hardly bothered to listen to him. She was more than tired, that night, from the heat of the long day among the shadeless fruit bushes. She was oppressed by the heaviness of the atmosphere.

There was a storm moving in slowly from over the Firth, she realized, glancing up to the dark heavy piles of thunderclouds gathering overhead, and wished that it would break and wash the sky clean of its own uneasy brooding.

When the first fat drops of rain spattered down she hurried William inside, and from the safety of the house they watched the lightning forking across the sky, counting the seconds till the thunder broke and ducking with their hands over their ears when it came. The scattered drops of rain increased to a shower and as the thunder and lightning slackened off the shower grew into a downpour. The Others came one by one over to where she and William stood with their noses pressed to a windowpane and they all stared out at the heavy downpouring of water as if mesmerized by the force and persistence of its beat.

"The power of water is one of the greatest forces on earth." It was her father who had told her that once, and vaguely it occurred to her then that there must be something in all of them instinctively recognizing this and that was why they were all held staring in awe at the fearsome rush of rain battering on the earth.

"Mam didn't take her coat!" Moira's voice suddenly exclaiming aloud brought her thoughts sharply back to the kitchen. They all looked at one another in dismay and Aileen said, "It can't last like this, surely. It's bound to ease off."

"I'll take it down to her when it does," she offered, and the Others agreed that was the best thing to do. They knew she liked being out in the rain and they had more work to do than she had anyway, and so, when the rain did eventually slacken off they drifted back to the ironing and the other jobs they had left and she ran off down the sea-road with her mother's old black coat bundled under her arm.

She had to dodge and skip to avoid the great puddles strung out along the road and it was doing this that caused her to trip and fall heavily on one knee. The force with which she fell against the rough surface of the road jarred an exclamation of pain out of her, but she had no idea how badly she had cut herself till she examined her leg in the light of the next street lamp and saw the great ugly gash in her kneecap. By that time, however, she was too near Mrs. Benson's house to think of turning back home to have the cut seen to, and so she ran on, slower now because of the pain in her knee and dodging the puddles more carefully.

The windows facing on to the garden of Mrs. Benson's house were all lit up and light streamed out also from the wide-open front door. She ran up the drive, feet pounding loudly on the gravel, and made for the side of the house where there was a door in the wall shutting off the front garden from the yard outside the kitchen door. The handle turned in her grip but the door itself wouldn't budge, and she was still pushing and rattling at it in exasperation when she realized that it must be locked. She made a jump for the top of it, draping the coat over it ahead of her, but the scraping of her injured knee against the wood as she tried to pull herself up was too painful and she had to drop back down again.

As loudly as she dared then she banged on the door and called, "Mam! Mam!"

Nobody came. She had seen figures vaguely outlined behind the long net curtains on the kitchen windows as she hung at the top of the door, but nobody came and at last she backed away from the door in the wall and edged along the house towards the front door. She could slip in there, through the hall and into the back premises; quietly, before anyone saw her.

The lobby inside the front door was carpeted. Her feet made no sound there but still she tiptoed from it on to the richer carpeting of the front hall. Now she was in the full light of a chandelier hanging in a blaze of prisms from the ceiling high above her head, but the hall was big, there were doors all round it and she didn't know which one of them would lead to the kitchen.

She took several hesitant steps towards one of the doors but a burst of laughter and voices—high English voices, raised suddenly behind it made her realize her mistake. In sudden, sharp terror of discovery she backed away towards the open door and escape from the trap she had blundered into, but when she swung round ready to bolt again she was brought up short by the reflection staring at her from one of the long, gleaming mirror-panels let in to either side of the front door. A white, startled face, her own face with rain-plastered hair clinging to it, gaped at her above a skimpy, rain-streaked trench coat skirting knees that were plastered with mud. And her right knee—oh, crivvens, just look at her right knee dripping blood all over the place!

In horror, she glanced down at the carpet under her feet. It was white, a soft furry white, but now there were patches of mud on it where she had trod as well as the accusing red specks of blood she had dripped on to it. She bent to brush clumsily at one of the muddy patches, and while she was still doubled over there was the sound of a door opening behind her and an astonished voice saying,

"Good God!"

She jerked upright towards the sound. Mrs. Benson and a tall, fair young man were standing as if they had just come out of the room from which she had heard the voices and the laughter. Mrs. Benson's face was redder than ever under the layer of white powder on it. It gleamed like a beacon of indignation at her between the long sweep of coffee-coloured lace dress and the tiara sparkling on her neatly corrugated grey hair. The young man's fair eyebrows were raised halfway up his pale forehead and he was looking at her with a kind of amusement in his face that made her flush as red as Mrs. Benson. As the coffee-coloured lace bore down on her he said,

"I must say, Madge, this is your most original party-piece yet!"

"Shut up, Claude!" Mrs. Benson wasn't amused.

"What the hell d'you think you're doing here?"

The words fairly hissed out of the red face at her, but so deeply was she shocked at hearing a lady swear that her sense of outrage was momentarily as great as Mrs. Benson's. With equal indignation she snapped,

"I only came with my mam's coat!"

209

Then she remembered about the stains on the carpet. Her rage deflated and she said humbly, "I'm awfully sorry about the carpet, Mrs. Benson. I couldn't get in the back way, you see, and I forgot about my knee."

"Your knee?" Mrs. Benson looked sharply down at it and turned equally sharply away.

"Oh, my God—Get it out of here, you little horror, *get it out!*"

"But where—"

"Calm, calm, Madge darling!" The young man, his arm round Mrs. Benson's shoulders, cut across her bewildered question. He moved over to a bellpush in the opposite wall and jabbed it with his finger. Coming back to Mrs. Benson his eyes raked her up and down and with a slight shudder he commented,

"It *is* a bit of a bloody mess, what!" But it wasn't to her he was speaking, it was to Mrs. Benson.

A door so smoothly fitted into the panelling of the wall that she realized immediately why she had missed it at first, swung open as he went back to his soothing of the coffee-coloured shoulders. Her mother came out, a tray in her hand, her face turned enquiringly towards them. She had on a white frilly apron and there was a white, frilled cap on her smooth dark hair. She looked like a parlourmaid, not like her mam.

Mrs. Benson's voice saying loudly, "Get this brat out of here, Mrs. McShane—I'll speak to you about this nonsense later," came over her mother's exclamation of

210

astonishment and the "Bridie! Oh, my lamb, you're hurt!" when she saw her knee.

Now they were all red-faced, she thought grimly; herself, Mrs. Benson, and her mother—all except the young man watching her and her mother with that look of disdainful amusement on his face. She looked back at him once as, in a flutter of apologies to Mrs. Benson, her mother pulled her away towards the kitchen door. The look was still there.

She thought of it all the time her mother and the cook were bathing and exclaiming over the knee. It had measured both her and her mother, that look, and the measure of it had taken all dignity away from them —made them seem like the poor people of the joke-drawings in the old copies of *The Quiver* they had at home.

Poor people never had any dignity or human feeling in these drawings. They were just supposed to be funny, always getting drunk or doing vulgar things or not speaking proper grammar. They weren't really people at all, in fact. They were just creatures who happened to have a comical resemblance to human beings without having any of their thoughts or feelings.

Her father had hated these drawings. They were an offence against social justice, he used to say, and now she knew what he meant and why they had made him so angry. The way that young man had looked sneeringly at her mother—her good, brave, gentle mother!—

211

as if she was a lower form of life than himself just because she was poor—*that* was an offence against social justice!

"Are you all right, pettie? I'm not hurting you too much, am I?"

Her mother, head bent down over the injured knee, was talking to her as she knotted the ends of the bandage. She couldn't answer her at first for the rage that was rising fiercely in her throat. That man wouldn't have dared look at her mother like that if her father had been alive, he just wouldn't have *dared*! Her father wouldn't have seen a sneering fool like that in his road!

Impulsively she reached out and touched the smooth dark wing of hair curving out from under the silly scrap of frilled linen. Her mother's head came up with a questioning murmur and as their eyes met she said earnestly,

"That man, Mam—all those people in the big houses. Don't you mind them. They're the kind of people Dad just wouldn't have seen in his road."

Her mother looked at her in blank astonishment at first, then the light of remembering came into her eyes. She bent down to the bandage again without answering, but after a moment she said,

"That's how I try to think of it, Bridie. But it's not easy."

Her hands, all bleached and wrinkled with the dishwater, gave a final pat to the bandage and as she rose to her feet she asked quietly,

"What made you say a thing like that, Bridie?"

There was the proper explanation, the story of all those long, hot summer days tangled up with guilt and remorse and the way some remembered words of her father's had made yet another thing clear to her. But the only part of it that was worth telling, the part she had thought would be so difficult, was easy now. She said it loudly and defiantly, daring the cook working a few feet away from them to laugh at her.

"Because I'm proud to have you for my mam. You're better than any of them."

Her mother and the cook both laughed, but it was a nice kind of laugh not embarrassing at all. *In for a penny in for a pound, it's love that makes the world go round,* the cook sang in a cracked voice, rolling her eyes up at the ceiling. She slipped down off the chair joining in their laughter at the cook's comic effort and under cover of it she said to her mother,

"I do still love you, truly, Mam."

It was so easy to say that too, and such a relief to have got it out at last, that she was astonished to find herself suddenly crying as freely as she had been laughing the moment before. But it didn't matter somehow, for her mother's arms were round her and it seemed she was just as happy either way.

8

There were two years at the Wishart for her after that during which, her mother said, she "settled down and learned to get on with people."

It was because all the other girls around her were forming special friendships at this time that she felt she wanted to do the same. It made her feel lonely and left out when she saw them going about in twos and threes with their heads together giggling over secret jokes and making private signs to one another in class, and she very quickly learned that the way to make special friends was not to go off dreaming by herself into some quiet corner of the playing field or to try and dominate all the others in her year. She had to give up some of her private thinking time, clamp down a little on the inclination to make everyone follow her like sheep before Jenny Lindsay and Ena Wallace accepted her as one of the little group she eventually made with them.

She had to be very careful not to seem odd or different to other people in her conversation with them, of

214

course, but it was worth it in a way. Jenny was very good at sports and Ena was the prettiest girl in the first year. She herself soon got a reputation for her ability to talk them out of any trouble they got into and so their group had a prestige that was very enjoyable.

There was still plenty of opportunity too, in spite of all the time consumed in the gossip and giggling of their conversations, to store away in the quiet, thinking part of her mind a whole rich gallery of impressions of the two years she spent at the Wishart: people's faces, their mannerisms, all the moments when, from being a participant in some incident, she would suddenly be caught up in an odd awareness of the people and things and atmosphere of which it was composed.

As if she was on a different plane then, another level of living entirely from the moment as it existed for those taking part in it, she would see it suddenly projected with a strange, objective clarity in front of her. And with a thrill of triumph she would know that she had snatched yet another moment from the wasteful stream of living running past her; another moment of time had been caught and petrified forever in her memory.

She could never have spoken to Jenny and Ena about all that, of course, never have risked their laughter at such imaginings, but in spite of that it was still very pleasant to be accepted, to have particular friends at last. Later on too, because they all came from the same village, it helped to make up for missing the Others.

Nell had gone off to be a kennel-maid at Blair Castle even before she started her first year at the Wishart, and a few months later Moira was sent as an apprentice to a dressmaking firm in Edinburgh where she lived in a hostel belonging to the shop. Aileen, who still wanted to be a doctor but of course there wasn't the money for that, decided to be a nurse instead. She left the Wishart too, at the end of her second year, and lived-in at a hospital in Edinburgh doing a clerking job in the Matron's office till she was ready to start her probation.

That left only William and herself at home by the time she went into her second year. It was strange then, without the Others. She hadn't realized she would miss them so, especially bossy Nell, but her mother said that living-in jobs solved so many problems that it was the best thing for all of them.

"If your father had lived it would all have been different," she kept telling them, and every time her mother said that—almost as if she was defending herself against charges they never made—she thought of her father swaying on his heels as he looked up into the canopy of leaves on John Knox's tree and swearing that, as he was a living Irishman, she would get a decent education.

Maybe he had said that to her mother too about the Others, and that was what was making her sound so defensive. She didn't know and never asked because she knew as well as they did that keeping them all eating their heads off at school till they were eighteen was impossible, even if they could have been sure of grants to the University at the end of it. They had to get out and earn—pull themselves up by their own bootstraps, as her father would have said.

All the same, she couldn't help envying Cissie Black and Jean Bailey and all the others who talked so glibly about "going up to Varsity," for she was as good as they were at some subjects and better at English than any of them. And sometimes, when they were particularly uppity about taking the Latin course while she was only in the Commercial, she really hated them.

Most of the time, however, she was happy at the Wishart. It was good to have friends, good to have interesting work to do, good to have an English teacher like Dr. McIntyre with his deep, rolling voice and a delight as keen as her own in the everlastingly beautiful complex structure of language.

He had a way of stopping suddenly at some line in a poem and repeating it to himself softly, as if he wanted to hear it again with a different, inner ear that would discover more meanings in the words, more tones in their sound than a first hearing could possibly give. If she had dared she would have followed along the same path of enchantment as openly in class as she did when she practised this trick by herself at home. But she didn't dare, and so she contented herself by closing her eyes and letting his voice draw the shape and colour and the tone of the words out of the air for her again; and so, it was not till he had been taking their class for a long time that she realized the effect this habit of his had on the rest of the form.

It was in the Shakespeare lesson that she stumbled on the truth. *"The uncertain glory of an April day,"* Dr. McIntyre had just quoted, and then he paused with the words, she sensed, still rolling round and round in his mind. His face was rapt, his head back-flung with open eyes staring sightlessly at the ceiling.

"Uncertain glory . . ." He whispered it again to himself, then a little louder, "uncertain glory . . ." he repeated reverently.

The girl sitting next to her nudged her. She opened her eyes and with a feeling of shocked disbelief realized that not only her companion but the rest of the class was quivering on the brink of laughter. She felt the emanations of it all round her and shrank inwardly from the shock of outrage that would strike Dr. McIntyre if the secret laughter swelling in them should break openly against the lonely, vulnerable pinnacle of ecstasy which he was willing them to share with him. But the hilarity trembling on their lips and in their eyes did not quite dare to break into open sound, and when the spell that was on him snapped suddenly it was to her that he turned with an expression on his face that she found oddly sad.

"There you are, little Bridie McShane, poet-in-embryo. Write one such phrase and you will at least be touched with greatness. You'll transcend your little shop-assistant's fate."

None of the rest of the class knew what he meant but she knew he was talking about her going into her grandfather's business at the end of that school year. She had told him about it just after it had all been arranged with her mother's brother, Uncle George, for Dr. McIntyre was her form-master and she had to let him know she would be leaving at the end of that term. It was only because he had questioned her so closely at the time, however, that she had admitted her desire to stay on at school till she was educated enough to write poetry properly, but once that was said she had been quite willing to let him see the ones she had already written.

She had expected him to say something about them like Mr. Miller had done, but all he did when he had finished reading them was to tilt himself back in his chair with his hands clasped behind his head and chant her name softly over and over again, like an incantation.

"*Bridie McShane . . . Bridie McShane . . . Bridie McShane . . .*"

The chant stopped abruptly. There was a long silence, then he said slowly, "You're the most damnably odd mixture of naïvety and perceptiveness I've ever come across. There's a—dammit, what's the word—a kind of innocent wisdom . . ."

Silence again, a long silence. His eyes slid sideways to her taking her in up and down, long black-stockinged legs, straight flat-fronted gym tunic. For a moment of unbelieving alarm she saw in them a flicker of the look that had used to terrify her in fat Mr. Ferry's eyes. It passed so quickly that she thought she must have imagined it, and in his schoolmaster's voice again he said,

"I see you have a quotation from Marvell's 'To His Coy Mistress' scribbled on the flyleaf of this juvenilia. You're fond of this poem, are you? What d'you make of it, heh?—a love poem like that."

It was only the two lines, *"But at my back I always hear, Time's wingèd chariot hurrying near,"* that had ever meant anything to her. She told him so without, as she had to Mr. Miller, attempting to explain why, and he pounced on the confession.

"Ah-ha! So that's the key, is it, the key to all this fatalistic rambling about Time and Death and Eternal Circling? Not that the phrasing here and there doesn't show a fair degree of aptitude, but that is not the point. The point is how did you attain this, what is popularly called "poetic insight" into the significance of the moment, because—" He was thumping the desk with his forefinger now, softly emphasizing the rapid flow of his words. "—because such an experience, if experience there has been, can only be constructive if the subject of it succeeds in building *outwards* from it. Otherwise, there is only a self-destructive burrowing-inwards, a futile self-consumption of intellect that is the antithesis of creativeness. For creativeness, my child, is all outgoing. It is experience absorbed and put forth again in a finer form. You have followed me so far?"

She thought she had but the rapid way he spoke had made it sound rather complicated, and so she contented herself with a nod in reply.

"Then what," he asked in a milder tone, "what was this experience that has caused you to be so conscious of the thing Marvell expresses so aptly in his imagery of Time's pursuing chariot? Let us see whether you are only inwardly obsessed by it or whether, having accepted it as part of the fabric of your experience, you are now attempting to build consciously, creatively outwards from it."

Dr. McIntyre wasn't like Mr. Miller—he hadn't known her father, hadn't known both of them together. She couldn't tell him, as she had told Mr. Miller, of that day in the lane after Bluey's funeral. It would sound fanciful, contrived, like something she had made up instead of something real and painful she had lived through. It probably wouldn't even make sense to him unless she went right back to the beginning of everything about herself and her father, and she didn't want to do that.

"Everyone's entitled to a private place in the mind," her father had told her. Surely this was hers? Surely she could work out the meaning of what Dr. McIntyre had said without letting him into it?

"If you don't mind, sir," she said blushing at her own evasiveness which she felt sure he would despise, "I'd like to think about it a little more first."

"Do, my child, do." He nodded, apparently not put

out by the way she had slid out of answering him. "Poetry, *true* poetry is an art that will bear a great deal of thinking before one decides to make a vocation of it. And incidentally, much as I deplore this snatching of a bright pupil from the bosom of Minerva to that of Mammon, I would counsel you to look on it as no more than a stumbling block to your acquisition of learning. Consider all those men of letters, my child, who had little of what we understand as formal schooling. Take heart from their example and—to hark back to our earlier thesis on creative writing—remember that, as with experience, so with knowledge; it is not the manner in which you acquire it that matters, but the use to which you put it."

She had been about to go then with the usual murmured formality of "Yes, sir. Thank you, sir," when he stopped her and said in a hesitant, rather embarrassed way,

"Your—er—your father, Bridie—I believe he was a comparatively uneducated man?"

She muttered agreement, ready to bristle up defensively at anything else that might be said, but he only nodded, "Ah, yes. So I had heard. But by all accounts he was also quite an outstanding figure in some ways." And with a dismissive smile and a wave of his hand that terminated the interview he left her to figure out his meaning for herself.

He had intended it for comfort, she decided later. In fact, he had only been emphasizing his point about formal schooling not being so important by reminding her in a roundabout way that her father had pulled himself up by his own bootstraps. And what her father had done presumably, Dr. McIntyre had meant, she could do also if she put her mind to it.

Well, that was easier said than done, especially considering how little she really knew about the kind of man her father had been! Mr. Gladsmuir said he had been an atheist. Mr. Miller had once called him "a frustrated man of letters." Once, long ago, Major Morrison had shouted angrily that he was "a bloody Red." Mr. Purves sometimes told her that she had a tongue on her like her father's and that *he* could charm the devil himself when it suited him.

But where in all this was the man her mother had held up to them for years as a model of all the domestic virtues? *Your father wouldn't have approved . . . Your father wouldn't have permitted . . ."* That was the whip she had been using to keep them all in line for years now whenever her own gentler methods failed, scourging them with the wishes of a dead domestic tyrant.

And where, in all these other people's versions of the man her father had been, was the jovial, laughing man who had taught her all those hilarious Irish songs? The proud man who had taught her the meaning of courage? The gentle man who had sung the sadness quietly out of her as the sun's gold died into the darkening waters of the Firth? Where was all the warmth and strength she remembered and all the tender love that had wrapped her round so closely? What sort of man had he really been that she should still miss him so much after all these years—nearly five now, since he had died.

There was no answer. There never was any answer when she thought like this. There was only that prospect of the end of her ache of yearning for him that she still believed in somehow, even though she was so much older now than on the day Mr. Miller had told her it would be all right when she was grown-up. She could always rely on that to release her from this endless circling of her thoughts, back into the ordinary world of home and school and friends.

And William of course. She tended to forget about William nowadays because being at different schools meant that they saw so little of one another through the day. That last term she was at the Wishart, however, she was glad she still had him to fall back on for company in the evenings, for by that time she was seeing very little of Jenny and Ena after school. There were no more of the threesome walks they used to have and very little of visiting now in one another's houses—not since the other two had taken to joining the group of boys and girls who spent their evenings hanging around the Market Cross, talking and giggling and skylarking about.

She had been hurt at first by their defection from the routine the three of them had followed for so long, and she felt so lonely without them also to begin with that she had tried to join in with the Market Cross crowd and share in the fun they were having. Well, it seemed to be fun anyway, to anyone outside it as she was, but when she had worked her way into the group it turned out to be really very boring. The boys did nothing but tell dirty stories and the girls giggled and slapped them and told them to be quiet. Then the boys pretended to be angry at the slapping and grabbed the girls and wrestled with them and there was more giggling and guffawing, especially if a girl fell in the wrestling and the boys saw her petticoat.

It was all so disappointingly stupid that she felt quite angry with the other two for wanting to be part of it, but if they preferred to waste their time like that she certainly wasn't going to copy them. She could have much more fun with William playing on the rocks down at the beach or up in the woods round the farms, or even just talking to him. He was really very intelligent, after all, for ten years old.

He was a terrible boy to argue, too. William would argue the hind leg off a donkey, her mother said, but that only made him the more delighted to have her company again because, he said, she was the best arguefier he knew. They talked their way along every path in the woods round Redmains and Castlebrae and Castlemains that summer term, talked about anything and everything under the sun that could give them a good argument. The only times they were quiet were when they were spotting birds' nests in all the places

Nell had shown them when William was still such a little boy that he couldn't be trusted to keep secrets, or when they had separated to collect the driftwood they were supposed to bring home for the fire from their walks along the beach.

There were times that she shirked this job, for towards the end of that term she was troubled with vague uneasy pains in her legs and back that became worse if she tried to lift anything heavy. "Growing pains," her mother called them when she complained. They would soon go, she said. But they didn't go, they got worse, and one evening when she and William were walking home with the driftwood piled on their backs she was seized with such a spasm of the pain that she staggered against the fence at the side of the road.

She held on to the stakes of the fence, letting the driftwood slide off her back. William fussed round her but she was only vaguely aware of his voice piping anxiously in her ear for something was happening to her, something so bewildering and alarming that she could think of nothing else. She brushed him aside.

"Bring my wood," she said rapidly. "I'm going home myself," and left him, running as hard as she could for home.

Her mother was in the kitchen. She could see her sitting at the fireside sewing as she dashed up the front path. Her voice rose, calling out a question at the bang of the front door, but she ignored the voice and dashed into the bathroom. With fingers trembling so that they could hardly grip the stuff of her clothes she examined herself, and the first whimper of fear that broke from her at what she found grew into a panic-stricken shout.

"Mam! *Mam!*"

Her mother appeared in the bathroom door. "Good heavens, Bridie, you were running like a—" ⸱

"Mam—look! Look at me! What's wrong, Mam? What's happened? What is it?"

Even in her panic she saw something odd in the cautious, wary look that crossed her mother's face. She said slowly,

"Don't you know? Did none of the girls ever tell you?"

"Tell me what? Mam, what's *happening* to me?"

Briskly, brushing aside the clutch of her hands, her mother said, "There's nothing wrong with you. It happens to every girl at about your age."

The talking, explaining, went on till she broke into it incredulously, "*Every month!* Every month for the rest of my life?"

"Well, till you're a good few years older than I am anyway."

Her mother was raking things out of the bathroom cupboard, quite calmly, apparently with no idea of the monstrous sentence she had just pronounced on her. She rejected it violently, struggling fiercely as if against a trap that had been sprung on her.

"I won't have it! I won't *let* it happen to me!"

"Don't be silly, Bridie."

Still perfectly calm, her mother was deftly slitting and opening a package she had brought out of the cupboard.

"Nobody likes it but there's nothing *you* can do to stop it. You just have to accept that you're grown-up now."

It didn't penetrate at first. It was only after her mother had sent her upstairs with a cup of tea and an aspirin and she was standing at her window looking down into the garden that she remembered and understood what had been said then.

"You're grown-up now . . ."

The cup began to shake in her hand. She put it down on the window ledge and leaned with her forehead pressed against the glass. Down below in the garden all the flowers within the range of her distorted vision blurred and blended in a background kaleidoscope to her thoughts. Red of roses, purple of Canterbury bells, white of dog-daisies. Red and white and purple. A memory of red *on* white and purple heaved and stirred in her mind. The blood—dirty white of lambs' tails and red of blood on the violets! Herself running madly away from the suffocating horror of her face pressed down into the blood and bits of bodies . . .

She tried to blank out the memory and others rushed in to fill the vacuum—a confused, shapeless mass of memories, nightmare visions of limbless men and human-faced beasts, of flesh cold and dead under her warm hand and a brown, laughing face clay-grey with

228

pain; of pain lying hot and hard and irremovably heavy in her chest. Strange words loomed out of the nightmare mass—*Life, Death, Time*—and stalked huge and meaningless through the chaos of her mind. And with the glass pressing coldly against her forehead she gave herself up to a despair that was endless and utterly, totally complete.

She didn't understand. She didn't understand anything any more. She was grown-up now but nothing had changed. There was still all this in her mind, trapping her, holding her down, haunting her with the terrible, inescapable knowledge that she had never asked for, never wanted. She was grown-up now but she was still feeling the same, thinking the same as she had always done. She would have to go on for the rest of her life thinking like this, running, running away from the sound of chariots, always afraid of Time catching up with her, of dying like her father had done.

". . . like her father had done . . ." She couldn't get away from that. She still missed him, still wanted him. Mr. Miller was just a dotty old fool after all. There *was* no last refuge. She was grown-up now but nothing, nothing, *nothing* had changed.

9

The station platform where she waited a month later to board the train that would take her to Grannie's in Edinburgh and her first job, had only a few people on it besides her mother and William and herself. July was the month in which people came to the village. It would be the beginning of September before the "up" platform was crowded again with holiday-makers taking the train home to Edinburgh and she was glad to be leaving at a time when there were no crowds to come between herself and her last look at the neat, Noah's Ark shape of the wooden station buildings, the borders of pink and white and parti-colored Sweet William edged so tidily with white stones. Now she would be able to remember the station properly, the way she had always known it.

Her mother was talking, repeating advice already given, as last-minute warnings and exhortations. She tried to listen but she was too uncomfortably aware of herself to pay any real attention. The corset her mother had said she must wear to "keep her figure in" was itching her. Her dress and coat were longer than anything she had ever worn before and when she moved she was very conscious of them flapping about her legs. Neither of them fitted very well because they had been made down from jumble-sale stuff, but it was more the unaccustomed shape than the fit that bothered her. And she was wearing a hat too, something she had never done before. The band round the inside of it was slightly too tight and she kept ducking her head to ease the constriction of it on her brow.

"Don't fidget, Bridie," her mother said. "You're not a child now, remember."

She straightened up, glancing enviously at William who still got to fidget. He was jumping back and forward over her suitcase, the same suitcase that Nell and Moira and Aileen had all carried in turn when they left home as she was doing. It rocked slightly every time his foot tipped it in a jump for it was as light for her as it had been for each of the Others. None of them had carried much more in it than a single change of clothes for the ones they wore on their backs.

Her mother checked him at last, but kindly, for William was still her baby though he came nearly up to her shoulder now. Strange that she should ever have thought of her mother as a big woman! She was quite small really, hardly any taller than herself. She had become plumper too, this past year. Her face had got back some of the round pinkness it used to have—in fact, she

231

was really quite pretty again with that little lilac-coloured collar on her black dress—not the old one, thank goodness! That had gone in the bucket the day Moira had come home looking very grown-up and competent with the big cardboard box under her arm and said firmly, "C'mon, Mam. Off with the old, on with the new!"

The ripple of advice was still going on at her ear, the same advice she had been given last night when her mother had sat on the edge of her bed, a humped black shape against the moonlight flowing in through the window. She was to try and love her job the way Nell loved working with the dogs at Blair Castle but she wasn't to be silly and flighty like her, always lovelorn over some stupid boy or other. Try to be like Aileen and keep her eye on the future. Never mind if the present was dull routine work, she would get her chance to shine one day like Aileen would when she was sweeping the boards of all the awards in nursing. (Poor Aileen, she had *so* wanted to be a doctor!)

And Moira—well Moira was a good girl for all she had refused to be tied down at the dressmaking and was wandering so footloose round the country from one hotel job to another. If it hadn't been for the money that Moira sent home—well, Moira was a good girl and if Bridie wrote home as often as Moira did she would be quite happy about her.

"Yes, Mam. Yes, Mam." She was agreeing, had agreed, with everything that was said. Only once, when her

232

mother was going over the characters of all the Others and saying how they had got this or that from herself or from their father, had she asked a question.

"What did I get, Mam? What did I get from you both?"

The hump of the black shape on the edge of her bed straightened up and became the silhouette of her mother with her face turned so that the line of her features was traced by the moonlight's soft, pale gold.

"Very little from me, dearie." The silhouetted lips moved smiling over the words. "We're not alike in our ways of thinking, you and I. But you got the gift of the gab from your father, you can be sure of that. And you have the same fire in you—the same great love of life that he had."

Her mother turned her head so that she was once again a black, faceless block of shadow, and after a moment she said quietly,

"But don't be proud of any gifts you have, dearie. Be grateful for them, remembering they are a trust from God that you must render back some day."

Then slowly, because her rheumatics were now so bad that it hurt her to bend her knees at all, she knelt down by the bed and prayed aloud to God to guide the fourth and youngest daughter of Patrick and Agnes McShane when she went out to face the temptations of the world, to guard her and have her in His keeping, for ever and ever, Amen.

William was interrupting now, piping up with questions about living in Grannie's house. Would Bridie still get to read Secular Literature on the Sabbath like they were allowed to nowadays at home? Would she go to the Meeting with Grannie and Grandpa and be Saved? Would she Cross over Jordan with the rest of the Brethren?

She smiled, remembering how much the question of being Saved had perturbed her when she was as small as William and, catching the twinkle that came into her mother's eye at the same time, realized suddenly how comical her seriousness must have appeared to the grown-ups round her then.

"Children have such literal imaginations."

Her mother turned her face away from William to murmur the comment smilingly to her and she nodded, smiling in reply. It was only briefly that their eyes held, but in the flicker of time it took for their mutual feeling to register on her mind she was sharply and pleasantly aware of a transition taking place within herself. Suddenly she was no longer a schoolgirl uneasily masquerading as a woman. She *was* a woman, a young woman sharing a secret grown-up understanding with an older woman.

The hoot of the train arriving, however, the fuss and bustle of steam, slamming of doors and shouting, gave her no time to think of the moment or to ponder its implications. She was on the train and in her carriage, the last good-byes said, the last kisses exchanged before she really knew what she was doing again. Her mother was a small, dark figure receding along the platform. William was only the bobbing up and down of a blond head beside her, and she was waving, waving frantically and calling out that she would write, that she would come home again soon, with the rush of the train whipping her words away and scattering them thinly down the wind.

The village dropped away behind her as tiny and unreal as the village of coloured cut-outs she had played with when she was little. The train rattled on into the mining country round the Wishart Institute. The great cone of the slag heap and the wheel of the winding gear above it flashed past, black against the red-gold westering sky. Then they were passing the Wishart with all its long lines of windows flashing golden at her and, as they were left behind, blinking out again one by one into cold grey glass.

The symbolism of the golden windows that had grown as blind and cold for her struck her suddenly with such poignancy that tears started to her eyes, but the current of her thought was too strong to be diverted for long by self-pity. She blinked the tears away and went on trying to fit the moment of communication with her mother on the platform into the pattern of her last conversation with Dr. McIntyre; the conversation that had taken place on the day she had handed in her class-books to him and left the school for good.

She hadn't wanted to talk to him—not really, not while she still felt so confused and trapped over what

235

had happened to her. There was a need stronger than her reluctance driving her, however, for there was no one else she *could* talk to. Mr. Gladsmuir would only have told her to pray for guidance, Mr. Purves would only have laughed and said, "Ach, stop wondering, Bridie. Wondering only makes your head big." And Mr. Miller. She hadn't seen Mr. Miller again, hadn't wanted to after that terrible letdown he had given her. And so she had tackled Dr. McIntyre, interrupting him in the middle of his kindly little speech of farewell as he took the pile of worn books from her.

"Sir, would you mind saying that again about creativeness? What it is and all that, I mean, and about absorbing things into the fabric of experience and putting them forth again in a finer form?"

"Ah yes, Bridie, we had quite a talk about that, hadn't we. *'Time's wingèd chariot'*—that was what started us off, wasn't it?"

"Yes, sir. That was it, sir," she told him, hoping he would say it all over again as he had before. And he did, but so much more slowly and quietly that she felt she had really grasped what he meant.

"You've had time to think it over," he reminded her when he had finished. "Do you want to tell me now what's troubling you? There *is* something, isn't there?"

"Yes, sir—but—it's difficult."

He gave her time, fiddling about with a pencil sharpener and not looking at her while she searched for the right words, but even then it was only a very simple,

236

halting effort on her part. He listened quietly, not interrupting or trying to help her out of her difficulties,
and the only time he looked at her was when she said,

"—and it's not any different now, even though I'm
—you know—grown-up. I still think about it all, about
my father dying and Time catching up on me. I still
feel alone. I'm still—afraid . . ."

"You always will be alone," he said quietly then.
"Alone in your mind, that is, for you have chosen the
loneliest of all vocations—or rather, I should say, it has
chosen you."

He rose and began to pace up and down the room,
in silence at first and then talking in time to his pacing.

"All men are afraid of the passage of Time carrying
them on to death, Bridie, but only to some in each
generation is granted this awareness of each passing
moment as a fragment of the totality of Life itself. And
of those who are so aware, there are only a few who
have the talent to express their awareness in some
creative form."

He stopped in front of her and sat with one hip on
the edge of his desk so that his eyes were level with
hers and gazing into them.

"The experience you had after your father died has
given you this awareness," he said earnestly, "but it's
not, as you seem to think, an end for you. It's only a
beginning, and in time—because you happen to be one
of the fortunate few to possess that talent for expression—you will learn, you *must* learn, to build con-

sciously, creatively outwards from it. And when you do you will find that in this, and not in forgetting or running away or trying to be different from the way that nature intended you to be, lies the comfort for your fear of knowing—the compensation for your loneliness of understanding."

She understood what he meant, understood it perfectly as she should be able to do at her age, but an earlier and much more childish feeling blocked her mental acceptance of it. She blurted it out, as childishly, bitterly, resentfully as she had always felt it.

"He *shouldn't* have died—it wasn't fair! He wasn't old, Dr. McIntyre, he wasn't old! And he loved life. My mother's said so, often."

"*Then live for him!*"

Dr. McIntyre slid off the desk as he spoke and stood looking almost angrily down at her.

"You are your father's daughter. He's in your brain and in your blood. Live for him! Don't let your talent die because he is dead. Let it flower from his death and speak for both of you!"

"Yes, sir," was all she said. "Yes, sir." And yet she was suddenly as breathless as if she had been running a race and as excited as if she had come in first. If only she could do that! If only she could! And then, remembering her manners as she backed out of the room, "Thank you, sir. Good-bye, sir."

She smiled now, in remembered embarrassment at the gaucheness of her departure, and leant her face against the window wondering what her mother would have thought of that odd interview. She would tell her about it some time—some time when she had got a little more used to being grown-up than she was now, and they would smile together over it the way they had smiled over William.

That was it—the link she had been looking for in the two things! The exchange of smiles that had told her she was on the same side of the barrier as her mother —the grown-up side of the barrier which cut the world of children off from that of adults. Her mother had been right. She *was* grown-up now whether she liked it or not but . . .

It was strange, she had never expected to feel like this. She liked it! It was the same as taking a deep plunge into the sea on a cold day—scared before she hit the water and then so exhilarated once the plunge had been taken that she felt she could swim until her fingers gripped the horizon and pulled her up over the rim of the world!

She stared out into the gathering dusk through which the train was rushing now, with the same breathless excitement as she had felt when Dr. McIntyre had told her angrily, "*You are your father's daughter—live for him!*"

She might be able to do that now she could look back and see everything that had taken place happening to her as it would to a child like William! She was thinking about it now as a grown-up would, after all, accepting it as something that had happened to her when she was a child. She tested the feeling, cautiously.

It still hurt, there were still tears inside her for her father, still a sound of chariots in her ears. But there *was* a difference about it all now that she was looking back on it as something that had happened *before* she was grown-up. She could see beyond it now, see into the future when she might be able to do as Dr. McIntyre had told her and "build consciously, creatively outwards from it."

The train pulled into Waverley Station and she got out into the black bustle of it clutching tightly on to her suitcase with one hand and to the purse in her pocket with the other, for her mother had warned her well about pickpockets. Clumsily dodging through all the unfamiliar hazards of the busy station, she made for the entrance. The thronging pavements, the noise, the sensation of being hemmed threateningly in by all the tall buildings, held her dazed for a moment. A woman barged into her and stepped back, glaring.

"I'm terribly sorry—I wasn't lo—" she began to apologize, but the woman only looked her up and down contemptuously and hurried on, muttering under her breath.

"It won't be like the village, remember," her mother had warned her. "They're in too much of a hurry for good manners in the city," and she tried to soothe the hurt in the contemptuous look by reminding herself of this as she walked to the tram stop.

It was almost dark now and she had never found her way to Grannie's house by herself before, but she knew which tram to take. She swung aboard it confidently, and climbing to the top deck went forward to the open, semicircular cabin in front. This was the position she liked best, swaying and rocking high above the shop-fronts and the garden walls. It was from here she could get glimpses of odd, unexpected things. It was up here, holding on to the brass rail in front of her that she had the feeling, the strange and thrilling feeling of plunging forward at the helm of an immense, unstable galleon over perilous seas.

The tram jerked into motion and she leaned forward devouring the city with eager eyes. The noise, the traffic, all those people swarming everywhere—it was like an immense version of the little fair that came to the village every year! And all those huge buildings hemming everything in, the tall shop-fronts, the long-sprouting chimneys, the giant church spires spearing the sky—everything was on such an enormous scale! It would take her years to explore everything, years and years.

The tram began an upward climb that took it away from the city centre and out towards the quiet suburb where Grannie lived. The long street that led to the terminus sloped down from the other side of this gradient. It was a quiet street, dark and narrow, with no traffic to disturb it at this hour, no people walking its pavements; a street where nothing should have happened. Yet suddenly, in the unlit window of one of the tall houses gliding past her she saw a great vase of full-blown roses, white roses looking with soft, ghostly faces at her out of the purple-black darkness of the empty room behind them.

Then they were gone and she was staring down at the pale pools of gold spilled from the street-lights on to the cobbles, staring along the tram-tracks running in thin, cold-silver lines into an infinity of darkness at the end of the street. The last of the passengers had got off at the top of the gradient and there was no one but herself now on the lurching upper deck of the tram; no one in the street, no one in the world but Bridie Mc-Shane gripping the golden rail that steadied her at the helm of her galleon plunging through perilous seas. And in her head there was a poem moving, a poem that held the sudden ghosts of roses in the grape-bloom darkness of an empty room . . .

Summer's ghosts,
Sweet ghosts of all her summers . . .

As the dancing pattern of words began to take shape in her mind she thought of the book packed away in her suitcase, the book in which she wrote all her poems, and wished there was time to get it out before she reached Grannie's. There were so many ideas she wanted to write down then and there! But perhaps Grannie would allow her a light of some kind in her room for a little while before she went to bed. That was all she would need. A little light, a little time.